I0614285

China Deep

There is No Wind Thorough the Tress
On a Treeless Beach

Scott Shaw

Buddha Rose Publications

Cover Photographs by Scott Shaw.

ISBN-10: 1-877792-11-X
ISBN-13: 9781877792113

Library of Congress: 2009926191

First Edition 1990
Second Edition 2007
Third Edition 2018

10 9 8 7 6 5 4 3 2 1

Printed in the United States of America

China Deep

There is No Wind Through the Trees
On a Treeless Beach

Table of Contents

The sky it was placid blue. Not intense blue like in the South Pacific. Not hazy distant blue like in Mother India. Not smoggy blue like in L.A., Taipei, or Bangkok. But soft, caressingly gentle blue, like the feeling of the woman who sat next to me.

We held each other's hands, stared into each other's eyes—like in all the old romantic black and white B-movies. But, we were living this one in full color.

We were on the grounds of an ancient Taoist temple. A temple deep in the PRC, (The Peoples Republic of China). A temple that the government had long ago rid of all its holiness—excommunicated those who did not worship the State. They, the PRC, had destroyed it—gutted the temple, cast out all of the Taoist angels—dismissed them to the heavenly realm. Now, they, the PRC, had rebuilt it. For what reason, one could only guess. A temple by the sea. A temple where only the few who knew of its existence could travel to—go and walk among the fading mystic vibrations and dream the dreams of another time—a spiritual age, lived a long time ago.

We sat in a gazebo. A Taoist gazebo. A gazebo as the wind blew gently.

In the not too far distance there was the Divine Mother Ocean. Full in her own intensity. Complete in her own all-encompassing form. She reflected the perfect blue of the sky. I looked at the ocean and then I turned my eyes to the girl. I slowly leaned in towards her. I watched as her eyes softly closed. I gentle kissed her upon the lips.

The first kiss. The best kiss. The only one that ever really matters. For it may never be experienced again.

The kiss complete. It was perfect. Her Asian eyes opened: softly, slowly. She looked around. Was anybody watching, witnessing a Western man embracing a local girl?

Slowly her head pulled back from mine. She looked deeply into my eyes, like seeking the answer to the universe.

"Do you love me?" She asked.

All I could do was stare lovingly at her, feeling the perfection—the perfection of the universe as it fell precisely into my hands.

All that was ever desired was there within my grasp. My sorry existence was complete. Like the totality of a drop of rain entering into the ocean, I too had entered the divine abyss—fallen from one into the whole.

An unending moment passed…

"Can we walk down by the ocean?" She inquired.

I looked at her, smiled, and nodded, *"Yes."*

We stood up. She was tall, thin, long black hair—perfect poetry. And me, a stumbling dreamer, lost in a lost world.

We cautiously charted our way over the refurbished temple grounds, through side rooms and hidden courtyards, making our way to the sea. Careful with each step that no one would notice our movements or see our obviously in love images

8

wandering through the structure to the realms of the forbidden.

Hand-in-hand we made our way to beach. The sand was dense, yet not expansive. There were just a few feet between the sea and the plants which flanked the temple.

The waves were small, defined. The ocean held all of its wonder. Wonder that though I lived on it/beside it for most of my years, somehow its essence was still completely unknown to me. Unknown, until that point in time, that realization of love.

I stood there in awh. We stood there in love. I hugged her tightly. Her thin body intertwined so perfectly with mine.

My mind went to thoughts that I could not help but wonder, *'How strange destiny was. How bizarre life is.'* The things that had brought us together. Together, Ming-zhou and me.

The sounds of the waves pounded in my ears—merging from distant rumble to clearly defined concise individual movements. It was then that my heart was taken over—lost to the dream of love. Lost to her. Lost in China. And, I have never felt that way again.

Chapter 2

Thirty and forty: thirty years old and forty-thousand-dollars in debt. Yeah, the dreamer's life had caught up with me. You know how it goes: the journeys, the purchases, the temporary addictions to temporary women, and nothing slicing any good karma cash my direction.

I never really had a job. Not a job-job. Never really wanted one. I could never understand how people could throw away the short amount of time that we call life while making some owner-operator rich and free off of our hours of labor.

Well actually, I have done one or two things: ran a martial arts studio for several years, equaling little cash but a lot of babes. You know, the older sisters and/or the single or bored mothers of my younger students. Yeah, and I did a stint teaching at a University. But, the politics of academic life. Man, you wouldn't believe it. Did tons of *Karma Yoga* for this spiritual organization or that one. But, a job? No, never a real nine-to-five.

I guess it is not so much that I am against jobs, if they could only answer more of our true inner needs. I mean, for most people I guess they are good. Most people wouldn't really know what to do with their time if they didn't have a job to go to. I guess that's because they don't choose to live a life of creation.

The downside of the whole job thing is when people reach like sixty-five, seventy, or whatever, and then they retired. By then they're too old to really do anything and they die wishing that they had done more with their life. Me, a product of my generation, I guess, I always wanted to live.

And, I do mean LIVE. A thing like a job would just get in my way.

*   *   *

American Ph.D. background and expertise in management, organization, and education seeks position with Asian placement.

I took out said ad in this international newspaper which I would often read over Asia way: Hong Kong, the Philippines, Japan, Thailand, and the like.

*   *   *

I was in L.A. Stuck, no cash. My credit cards were relatively Max-ed out. Thus, the ad. Thus, the hope. Thus, the dream that maybe I would fall into one of those employment situations that would be more than meaningless.

So, enough of all the setup and all the personal definitions. I don't want to bore you here… On to the real stuff that the stories, the tales, and the dreams of dreamers like me are made of...

*   *   *

It was three days after the ad initially appeared—internationally speaking that is, that my telephone rang. It was just a bit past 1:00 in the PM. I was still asleep. Still in bed having consumed far too much grape the night before.

"Hello," my telephone was groggily answered.
"Yes, this is John Dozer of the American Financial Consulting Corporation based in Hong Kong and I

would like to know when would be a good time to speak with Spencer Saint James regarding employment with our firm. This conversation should take approximately twenty minutes."

I'm going to give it to you straight here. I'm changing the name of the dude and of the company for obvious reasons—which will become abundantly clear shortly. You know, *to protect the innocent and all...* Well, if there is such a thing.

Initially, I was a bit taken back by being awaken by an international telephone call. In actuality, based in my deep-rooted human pessimism, I had not expected to get any response from the ad I placed at all. *Was that being negative?* And, for sure, I thought that if anyone would ever actually make contact that they would definitely hit me with a letter asking for my resume via the old P.O. Box. But, a telephone call?

"Well, I guess now is about as good as time as any to discuss the situation," I told him.

Not wishing to be too wordy and essay-ive here. You know, like Hemingway used to write. When you have to try to figure out just who was actually saying what and doing what, and what was going on... So, I'm just going to condense the discourse here and give you the highlights.

Basically, the dude told me that the position would involve my relocating to Asia. Initially to Hong Kong. *'Cool!'* But, he was sketchy as to the exact final lo-cal where I was to end up, which made me a bit nervous. He said that post my initial indoctrination I would be somewhat on the move.

"Like a traveling salesman," I asked.
"No," he emphatically stated.
Confirming my specs, Dozer asked,

"Was I still single and unencumbered?"
"Yes."

I mean, *'Fuck,'* it had only been a few days since I had put the ad in... But then, I guess everything in one's life can change in an instant, as I was about to find out.

Of course, being the fine businessman that I am, I inquired as to what was going to be my pay scale.

"To be discussed," was the answer. But *"Lucrative,"* I was assured. And, all of my expenses would be taken care of.
"I only fly First Class," I exclaimed.

That seemed of little consequence.

*   *   *

No resume required and actually very few questions asked as to my experience and or qualifications. I didn't really think all that much about it at the time, being a bit overwhelmed in general by the hangover, the call and all. But, as I rolled back over in my bed to contemplate my move forward—to where I have long known I belong, living permanently in Mother Asia—the cynical, verging on the paranoid, trust-no-one street kid that I am, began to emerge.

His final question before he hung up,

"How soon could I be ready to leave?"
"One week."

Leave it to me to think that everything occupies so short a space of time and push myself up against the wall to the max.

*   *   *

That week. This first part of this story. Does it really matter? I don't know. Does life really matter? I don't know that either. I guess life is ultimately only important to the one who is living it and even then, sometimes it matters not.

Actually, I got right on it, however...

If I may discuss the prelude to this actual piece of literature just a bit more. I already had a storage unit on PCH, (Pacific Coast Highway), full of guitars, books, my paintings, and all of the junk that I wished I could fit into my small, on the beach, apartment. So, I went there, rented a second one—a second storage unit.

I won't bore you with the intensity of the hell of solo moving all the rest of my worldly possessions into that space of waiting. Let's just conclude, it was hell.

I kept the basic clothing out—my travel stuff. Packed it into my bad garment bag. That's all I took. I was going to Hong Kong. You can always find anything you need in Hong Kong.

I initially wanted to keep my apartment, but nine bills plus a month, there was no way I could pay that and live the dream out on the outskirts. So, stored, and packed. I was gone.

*   *   *

I got on the plane, First-Class. Forty thousand feet high. I had the stewardess hit me with a glass of the bad iced *java.*

As the plane flew to its destination, I was embraced with the fact, *'God, this is where I belong.'* Even as I sit here now and record for history the exploits of this story; I know it, I feel it.

Okay, Okay, end of the interlude...

Chapter 3

The city of Hong Kong, *damn,* it pounds hard. I love it there. I wish I were there now: the heat, the intensity, the poverty, and the wealth.

I picked up my garment bag from the baggage claim, changed a few U.S. dollar bills over, and made it for the taxicabs line. It was about 8:15 in the PM and I was about to enter into *The Twilight Zone.*

*　　*　　*

The Financial Consulting Corporation had me set up at this corporate apartment on the Kowloon side of Hong Kong. Its address had accompanied the DHL international express courier delivered air ticket which I had received a day or two the previous.

I had been there many a time, not to the apartment, but the city—Hong Kong. My taxi ride… I felt like I was leaving the womb, being reincarnated into the realms of a place I've known—going home after way too long a wait in the ethereal plane.

The taxi took me to the apartment building rising up into the Hong Kong sky. Met at the door by a Chinese doorman.

"You must be Dr. Saint James."
"Call me Spencer."

He took me to the flat—up the elevator, complete with the basic small talk that goes along with the ride.

"Is this your first time to Hong Kong?"

16

"No."
"Is there anything that I can do for you Dr. Saint James?"
"No. And, call me Spencer."

Me, I had my own plans. It was pushing a year since I'd last been HK way. I wanted to reintroduce myself to the HK night. I'm sure she had missed me.

So, I sent the doorman on his way. Hung up my clothing. Walked around the place; two bedrooms. I checked the other bedrooms closet. It was empty. Good, I was *a-liv'n* solo sort of guy— just not much into that social roommate sort of thing.

Post the basic check-outs. I was out. Out, onto the street. Out with the night. The dream, the people. I was home—reborn.

There's a little bar I frequent over in Central. A walk out the door, a taxi ride, I was there. The bartender remembered my poison, *Greyhound*: vodka and grapefruit. The drink of the gods.

I poured down maybe twenty or so. Staggered my way out onto the street. Got a taxi. Rode to the flat solo. I don't remember the doorman, though, no doubt, he was there.

*   *   *

AM, the telephone rang. I didn't want to hear it. It rang, it rang again.

"Just leave me the fuck alone," I blurted out.

17

My head was pounding. The phone rang some more.

It was morning. The light shinned in through the windows blurring all semblance of reality—too hot, too bright, too real.

Ring! I pulled myself from the bed after maybe the thirtieth ring. I walked to the living room, the location of said telephone—as my body, my mind, and my soul, spun.

"Hello."

It was John Dozer. He wanted me to come in at eleven o'clock. That was in the A of M, so we could discuss my new position.

"Well John," I kindly told him, *"I'm a little bit disorientated due to the jet lag. I believe it would far better if I were to come in a bit later, say four o'clock, as this is my first day here."*

He was agreeable enough. I put the telephone down. *"Fuck!"* Now I knew why jobs were *no-where's-ville Daddy-O.* Man, you had to be somewhere at some specific time.

As I walked back into the bedroom, I passed myself in a full-length mirror. My clothing still hung from my body. I had slept in them. Awh, nothing new about that. My long blond hair was in a million places all over my head. I badly needed a shave. *'Fuck, what had I gotten myself into? What had they, the American Financial Consulting Corporation, gotten themselves into?'*

I fell on the bed. I went back to sleep. When I woke up, still feeling none too pretty, it was about

2:30 PM. I knew I had to drag myself up and out and try to pull it together.

I hit the shower, caught a shave. My clothing had become a bit wrinkled due to the journey and even though they had been hanging up all night they were still a mess. So, I did the instant travel iron bit—hung them up in a full-on hot shower, steaming bathroom, and closed the door behind me.

Though I had drank vodka the evening last, (which is generally the no hang over drink), I was down for the count. I was way wishing that there was something which I could wet my lips with to take the edge off this head throbbing experience. You know, like hit the hang over cure: A two packet of *alka-seltzer* in a beer—washing it down three to five aspirin, (depending on the intensity of said hang over). Then follow that up with a large *Seven-Up* and a stiff cup of the *joe*. But nothing, *nada*. A fridge, unstocked. I mean, it did have stuff, but like, you know, it was real people stuff—like food. Never let it be said that I was a real person.

So, nothing to do but tough it out. I got into my relatively shower pressed clothing, combed back my hair into a ponytail. Looked at myself in the mirror and thought, *'What if they don't like? I mean, I'm probably not quite what they excepted.'* Then I realized, *'Hey, I'm in HK. If they don't dig me, I'll just go hit a hotel on the plastic passion, credit card side of the picture, and crib back for a few days and party. And, you never know what you will find...'*

Actually, in all truth, I kind of hoped that would be the case—that they would take one look at me: longhaired, too big and way too long and baggy suit, and just say, *"Bye-bye."*

Anyway, I made my way down the elevator. I was greeted at the door by another and/or new doorman. I thought that I would have to get a cab to head over to the office, whose address had also come Stateside complete with all the other employment info., and the like. But no, there was a car waiting. AOK.

It was black sedan style. The doorman informed me as to its presence. He opened the rear door for me to enter. The driver, a Chinese man,

"Hello, Dr. Saint James. To the office?"
I wanted to say, *"No, let's go hit some house of dreams and get fucked up instead."*
But, I just shook my head, *"Yes."*

En route, he attempted to make some basic convo. I was in no mood. We drove on through the daytime masses of HK: the cars, the buses, and the people. He took the underground, under-bay, under-tunnel, Kowloon to HK. We arrived at a modern office building in Central. It, like all the others, kissed the Hong Kong sky.

"Did I need help finding the office?"
"Was it on the register?"
"Yes, it was."
"Than, No."

Inside. Up the elevator. Floor number twenty-one. A lady at the desk,

"May I help you, sir?"
"Spencer Saint James."
"Oh yes, this way Dr. Saint James."

She took me through the central receiving passageway—double-doored. As we walked down a hall, there were workers: Western, Asian, sitting in cubicles, typing, writing, and talking on the telephones in various languages. Offices flanked us. Some had windows, exposing their occupants to views of the Hong Kong Bay below.

A fucking office, nine-to-five. No way in the fucking world was I going to latch myself up to one of those cubical desks. No fucking way in the world!

I already had decided to just say, *"Sorry. Thanks but no thanks. I'll get the air ticket money back your direction and I am out-a-here."*

She took me into a large office, more like a conference room actually; with a large table down the center of it. She suggested I wait and someone would be along directly.

The view from the window was *pump'n.* It had begun to rain in HK and the clouds filled the sky with their intense gray essence. Man, I love it. Why couldn't all life just be like this dream: the vision of the clouds, the rain, and the promise of the passion in the Hong Kong night? I remained staring...

Into the room, maybe five minutes post came a man with his shaking hand already extended. He was smiling and jovial. He wore a white shirt, black slacks, and a red necktie. He was probably forty or so. Had brown, with just a few hints of gray, hair.

"Hi, Dr. Saint James. I'm John Dozer."
"Nice to meet you."

I looked for a hint of disappointment in his eyes, a glimmer that may symbolize his dissatisfaction with my appearance. In other words, my easy ticket out. There was none.

"Sit down Dr. Saint James. The director will be here in just a few minutes to explain things to you more completely. So, how was your trip?"
"Okay, no complaints. And please, call me Spencer."
"You have been to Hong Kong before; yes?"
"Many times."
"So, I guess this city holds no new experiences for you then?"
"Always a dream waiting to happen..."

The meaningless small talk continued for a few more, when in walks a man—older maybe late fifties. Wore a white shirt, blue/brown necktie, had a bit of a gut on him.

"Spencer, this is Mr. Kotch, our director."
"Nice to meet you," He extends his hand.

Basic firm handshake, etc...
The director sat down at the head of the table. We, Dozer and I, sat on opposite sides. My view was of the rain and the dream of HK—just outside that window. Again, I wondered what I was doing there.

"Would you like anything to drink, Dr. Saint James," asked The Director.

Well, I did, but I choose to decline the offer. He opened up a file. He read,

"Spencer Saint James, born in Los Angeles, California. BA, MA, Ph.D. Father served in the Pacific during World War II. Deceased. Mother, a former corporate executive. Deceased. You have never been married, have no known children. You hold a seventh-degree black belt. Are relatively fluent in Japanese, Korean, Mandarin, and Cantonese. You have never paid taxes. You own no property. And, you are currently in debt to the tone of $43,573.49. You..."

"What are you, CIA?" I interrupted.

He put his file down. They looked at one another: Kotch and Dozer. Then, they both intensely turn their gaze to me.

Dozer firmly says, *"There are many agencies which are based in the United States Government other than the CIA, Spencer."*

"What's this all about?" I equally firmly inquire.

"This is just to let you know that there is little about you that we do not understand," voiced The Director. *"We are not pulling any punches with you. We know virtually everything there is to know about you. And we are still offering you the employment that you were seeking in a field which we feel that you are capable of handling."*

"Which is?" I rudely expounded.

"We'll get into specific later, once all of the preliminaries have been discussed."

"Why me?"

"Because it was you who were seeking Asian employment and you are unencumbered."

"You mean, I am expendable."

"We are all expendable. For some fewer tears would be shed and less questions asked."
"But, we don't anticipate that with you," chimed in Dozer, *"Your assignment will not be that dangerous."*
"My assignment?"

*   *   *

Anyway... Once again not to get too wordy here, I was recruited. They laid down a bit more about what they thought they knew about me. I realized that physical statistics of one's life never truly reveals who a person truly is. *'They didn't know me at all!'*

They told me of their organizational objective. All the basic nonsense. Hey, at least it wasn't an office job!

I was spared the details of what my actual assignment was to be. I was only informed that I would be relocated into a secondary realm of Asia and it would take approximately one week to complete the first mission. As for the payment, $10.000.00 per month, divided by fractions there-of. As for my training, *"What no commando training,"* I inquired. No, due to my martial art ability and my being in fairly good physical condition, I would need none; simply a one-day briefing period, the day prior to my departure.

They told me to relax for a few days—get used to the time zone, for soon I would be on my way. Well, relax, that is not exactly what I had on my mind, if you catch my meaning.

*   *   *

I was driven back to the apartment. My mind was spinning. Now that the spinning from the drink had subsided, it was currently induced by another form.

As I walked into the building, I was greeted by the original doorman. As I rode up in the elevator, I could not help but wonder, *'Did they own this entire complex. I would have to check that out,'* I thought.

Inside the flat, I walked around a bit—lost. Looked out of the windows. Looked in the vacant rooms; the empty closet, the refrigerator.

Nothing to do, nowhere to go, or should I say, nowhere to run. I lay down on the bed.

*   *   *

Going to Asia I never suffered that severe of a jetlag. I guess, due to the fact that I generally stay up very late in L.A. Sometimes though, on the second day there, it was sleep-city. This was especially the case after the fact of staying up very late on my first night of arrival. Anyway, this feeling of needed sleep was common to me—the emotions that were currently placed inside my head, were not.

I set up my portable credit card sized alarm clock/calculator, purchased at a drugstore in Hollywood a decade before, to wake me in time for the evening's festivities. I was drifting to what I hoped would be a nap. The thought came to me once again, as it had when all the rap was being laid down my direction in the office, *'Where they, these dudes, this set up, really Americano. I mean, they could be sending me into anything. There was no way that I could even check them out. Part of the deal, you know, no telephono contact to the outside world as to what I was up to.'*

Expendable... What a great feeling to have/to know that you mean so little.

Chapter 4

The alarm rang. I turned it off. I didn't wake up from that nap, that day to that night. I was zoned. Awoke 4:00 AM, day next. Tried to go back to sleep, but that was no-go.

I thought to write in my journal, as I generally do—as to all of the goings on. I do that sometimes, you know, like when I wake way Asia early and can't catch anymore Z's. Then I realized that, *'Hey,'* I couldn't go for that either, the writing. You know, like they may confiscate the bad boy. In fact, I looked through it as to the words I had previously, in flight, placed upon the pages. I wondered had they already taken note of said writings and/or made a photocopy?

My poetry from the time—too personal, as well. This government agency stuff was not easy. So, I tore out the pages. Ripped them up. I mean like no paper shredder was at hand. I went to the head and flushed the torn pages down the toilet. I did all this as the song Johnny Rivers sang, *"Secret Agent Man,"* was going through my mind, *'Giv'n you a number and tak'n way your name...'* What had I gotten myself into?

*   *   *

Not being able to go back to sleep and it way too early to go out, I wondered around the place some more, trying to figure out some hint as to what was going on.

I looked. I looked closely. There was nothing. No smudges, except for the ones I had left, no lose or fallen hairs, no hidden cameras, or bugs in the telephone receiver, *nada.*

About 6:30 AM I decided to catch a little on the breakfast side of the picture. I went to the refrigerator. I was pulling a few things out and then I began to think, *'I wonder if this stuff is drugged.'* I guess I had seen too many James Bond movies. Paranoia holding tight, I decided to go and hit the out-side and eat somewhere a bit more potentially safe.

I deemed it an appropriate enough time to go out and cruise the HK streets.

I got dressed. Hit the elevator. Riding down with me was a local HK lady, maybe forty. I wanted to ask her if she was on the *Agent Operative Tip* as well, but thought I better just sit tight.

Met by the doorman, to no consequence, a hello and out to the streets I went.

*   *   *

Hong Kong was already pounding. Hong Kong is forever pounding, twenty-four-seven hours of a lifetime. People were all going somewhere. I decided not to ride but to hoof it. I love to power with the people in the morning.

I walked it on over to Wan Chai, in the heat, in the humidity. Sat back, had some morning cappuccino in this little, way overpriced, inner building, inner-mall cafe that I knew. I watched the babes go by.

It was pushing ten by the time and I was fully up and about. I grabbed the subway, hit over to Central, walked down the street, looked at a few Rolex dealerships, thought to pull out my plastic passion and hit myself up with another one of those bad pups. But, I chilled back.

It was a funny feeling, you know. I had nowhere to go. I walked around, but it all felt so empty. I don't know, it was a feeling I had in HK before. Like there's just so much going on, so many babes I would love to party with, so many millions of dollars: HK, U.S., and otherwise that I would love to possess. I mean everything is there: the babes, the fashion-passion, the money, enlightenment in the streets; everything. But, for some reason, at times, it's like being on the outside looking in—there seems to be no way to grab a hold of it.

I mean, sure, a babe will check me out here or there, but I mean, like, how do you make that contact. HK life—it all was at a distance. Distance, how could I bring it in close?

*　　*　　*

The day pushed through to the night—as the days of life tend to do. I had spent the majority of it back; set up at crib central wondering just what the fuck was going on. I had napped but refused to let myself waste another night in REM land.

Ready and out, I hit the streets. Hit my bar, then a subway ride to my dance club of choice on the Kowloon side. You know, there are so few dance clubs left in Hong Kong. As karaoke had swept the world, they had instantly replaced them. But, if you ask me, God has cursed the earth with two things, Theatre and Karaoke.

So, a search constantly ensues, find the remaining dance clubs of Asia. I hit mine. I met a girl. And, you know how it goes, the distance was distant...

    *   *   *

I was laced. I don't even really remember getting back to the crib. She was tattered up on the intoxicated side of the picture, as well—a serious babe: Chinese, twenty-five-ish, caramel colored skin, and sex that would drive a holy man to sin.

Post the passion, morning rolled around. My head spun. I had mixed the drinks the night before. I was going to be way sick.

I look over at the babe. I thought to wake her from her beauty sleep, go down on her one more time. But, I was feeling none too pretty.

I wondered if they, these people—the ones that were putting me up, would be pissed that I had brought a babe back to love crib central. I kinda hoped that they would. Maybe they would kick me out. Fire me before I was hired. Maybe they wouldn't want me anymore. Maybe...

I lay there. The phone rang. *'Oh shit,'* I thought. The babe moved around a little, as I lay there staring into the other room. Five, six, seven times. *'Fuck, I have to get it.'*

It was Dozer. Today was my day. I was to come in ASAP.

"Look my man, I am way fucked up. I have one kill hang over going on. And, I woke up next to this babe that I don't even know her name."
"I feel for you, Spencer. I have been in similar situations myself." He was attempting to be nice. *"But destiny does not wait. It is imperative that you come in immediately. Don't worry about the woman, leave her sleeping; we'll have someone come in and take care of her. Immediately, Spencer! You must come immediately!"*

He was nice about it, but very direct. A lot of thoughts went through my mind, like should I just tell him to fuck off. I mean the truth was, I was way more than nervous about the whole thing—out of my league, to say the least. Then, I thought of the life, the experience, and the illumination that comes from dancing into the hands of destiny, shaking hands with the devil —again. The book that I could someday write—if only I lived. And destiny, yeah, what did he mean by that anyway?

Destiny, huh? He did say the right word...

*   *   *

To make a long story short, I mentally pulled myself together, though my body was feeling none too well. I caught a shower. As I did, I made the whole thing, the whole feeling of nervousness, like a game. I watched it come and go, sought its source. Pretended that it was not there. And instantly, it was gone.

Out of the shower, I pulled on my baggy blue Italian suit, a blue print shirt, and a blue necktie. I knew I was still drunk as I fell over while trying to put on my shoes. Not the first time that has happened... But, I got it together, more or less, and threw that one last good-bye kiss in the direction of my nude golden skinned sleeping HK goddess. Damn, I wanted to fuck her one more time. I made my way down the elevator. I was met by the previously stated doorman and the same said driver who had motored me before.

En route, he attempted to make the same nothing conversation which he had previously. Again, I was not in the mood.

In HQ, Building-Central, I somewhat staggered my way up to the twenty-first floor. I was again escorted in by the front desk lady in waiting. This time I was taken into another office, a bit smaller, but still conference style.

There sat a man, probably my age, but looking much older. He wore a cheap suit and was probably fifty pounds overweight.

"Hi, I'm Jeff."

He extended his hand. I just looked at it.

"They got any coffee around here?" I asked.
"I'll bring you some," sounded off the front desk girl.
"AOK, hit it with a lot of sugar. Make it black."

I sat down in the large leather, head of the table, brown conference chair. I let my head lean back. My eyes closed beneath my round, mirror lens sunglasses. I was not in the mood for conversation. Maybe the plump boy caught my vibes. He didn't say anything. I was out-a-there. I went to sleep.

I felt a hand on my shoulder, I jerked as I awoke. It was Dozer.

"How you feeling Spencer?"
"Fucked!"

I noticed a cup of the forty-weight sat in front of me. I reached for it. Then, there was a sound, a clearing of the throat sound. I looked, it was the big boss man and he wanted his big boss man chair.

I twisted my neck around a bit, got my circulation going, slowly grabbed my cup of mud and sliced my way over to an apparently more appropriate seat. He sat down.

He plopped a file down on the desk and gave me this nagatory glance. *'Hey, what did they expect, hiring a guy like me sight unseen from the newspaper?'*

"We are going to discuss the assignment. I trust that you are up to it, Dr. Saint James."
"Actually, I'm not up to much of anything. But, I suppose that I have no choice. By the way, you got anything to fuck'n drink around here?"
"If you are attempting to discourage us about you Dr. Saint James, it is to no avail. We have checked you out thoroughly, including your obvious aptitude for the unsavory. So, pull yourself together and let's get down to business!"

I felt like saying, *"Fuck you"* to the old guy. In any other circumstance I probably would have. But, this was their ball game and I doubted that there was little that they could not control—including my living or dying. So, I just sat back.

I could see by the look in his eyes, that he, The Director, was pissed. I had instantly made a new enemy. *'Cool!'*

The Director looks at Jeff,

"Get Ms. Chang to get Dr. Saint James something to drink."

Jeff looked at The Director, with a somewhat glance of disarray. But, got up from his chair and left the room.

33

The Director continued, *"You're going to leave today. You will be crossing the border and entering the People's Republic of China. You will end up..."*

Now, I'm just going to leave the final geographic location blank here—for time, destiny, and world politics. It is better that way.

"You will initially be traveling by train and you should arrive there at approximately 7:00 AM tomorrow morning. There you will be met by Mr. Bloom."
"Who's that?"
"Jeff Bloom, the man who went to get you the drink."

About then, Bloom reenters the room, no drink in hand. I was not pleased.

The Director detailed, *"Mr. Bloom will arrive via air before you. He is stationed there so knows the situation very well. Once in country he is the one who will be guiding you."*
"Guiding me?"
"Let's just say, explaining further what you are to accomplish."
"What do you expect me to do, man?"
"That's not important at this point."
"Yeah, it is important!" I exclaimed.
"Look Spencer," says Dozer, *"We would not intentionally put you into a situation that would mean your harm or have you do something that is against your moral code."*

I don't know, did that ease my perception of this currently reality spinning in my head or not. *'What morals,'* I thought.

About this point, in walks Ms. Chang, (the front desk lady), a bottle of *Dom Perion* in her hand. She shows it to The Director and asks,

"Will this be Okay?"
"Ask Dr. Saint James," he responds in a disgusted tone of voice.

Me, I played it cool. First, I looked at the year.

"1968. Not a great year. But, I guess it'll have to do."

I give her a little smile and a wink. I began to crack the bottle open.
Looking up, Bloom obviously didn't dig my moves. *'Fuck him too,'* I thought.

*   *   *

The discussion continued to basically a whole lot of nothing.

"Get Dr. Saint James a glass," he instructed Bloom.
"Not necessary."

I took a slam right out of the bottle.

*   *   *

As my senses cleared with the flow of the liquid poison into my circulatory system and the zero *convo* continued, I inquired,

"Don't I get a gun or anything?"
"No, Spencer. We do not anticipate that will be necessary and besides it's very illegal to have a gun in the PRC. We don't wish to incur any unnecessary conflicts with the government that you will be the guest of," calmly proclaimed Dozer.
"Then why are we even in there," as I hit the bottle again.

The Director firmly moves his two cents forward,

"Dr. Saint James, we recruited you specifically for your command of the language and your expertise in hand-to-hand combat. Thus, we do not believe you will have any need for any additional weapons."
"What about like a radio transmitting device, if I need help or you guys to come and get me, or something?"
"You have seen too many movies," replies Dozer.
"Well, do I get like a badge or something?"
"No, absolutely not. We certainly do not want to bring any unnecessary attention to you," exerts The Director.

Well fuck me; there went all the ego stroking stuff. Like to flash a badge and say, *"Book 'em Dano, Murder One."*

*   *   *

The conversation was basically over. I still didn't know shit about was going on. They probably wanted it that way. But, *The Dom* had gone down nice and I was feeling way better.

"You will leave from here, now."
"Now?"
"Yes, now!"
"What about all my stuff?"
"It will be waiting for you upon your return."
"Really fucking great, guys!"

I needed another help cure the hangover shower. My clothing was none too happening. And, I was in no mood for train trip'n.

"Here is the passport that you will use."

It was filled with entry stamps, as if I had traveled to my destination country many a time. A photo of myself, looked quite recent.
'Where the hell had they gotten that,' I wondered? Samuel Storm was the name upon the page.

"Mrs. Chang will give you a small suitcase of necessary provisions and clothing."
"Will I like 'em?"

The Director stared at me for a moment. His growing distaste for me was obvious.

"They're a bit more functional than your current wardrobe. So, go take a shower, shave, and change

into the suit that is hanging in the shower room.
Mrs. Chang will show you were it is. Then you must
be on your way. It's getting late," proclaims Dozer.
"See you there," he concluded.

Bloom stick out his hand for a soul shake. I
looked at it. Fuck it and fuck me. I walk away.

Chapter 5

The ocean pounded softly upon the shore. I looked behind me, not quite on purpose, for I never look back, but I had turned just slightly to look into her eyes; the scene, the images, they caught me. It was almost too spectacular, too perfect. The ancient, now restored, temple slightly raised upon a hill. The colors: red, brown, and green, blending into the blue sky. Like a paisley acid vision, duped up on too much A. Like a Halloween night, I was fifteen years old, had eaten two hits of orange sunshine and one hit of purple haze. I traveled to Paris, to the moon, to mars—all while lying in my Hollywood bed, while the Who's song, *"I can see for miles and miles,"* continually replayed in my mind.

I was far away. I was too far away. I should have seen it, felt it all coming. I did, yes, I know that I did. I just didn't listen to myself.

I looked into her eyes. We held each other's hands. She wore blue. It blended with the sky. Her eyes, deep dark brown. Hair black like the night. Skin so pale.

I saw it. I knew it. Like some sort of *deja vu.* A moment known. I had lived it in a dream. Maybe on the train, maybe years ago—somewhere, somehow. Why, I do not know. But on the planes of existence, sometimes things are all a fallen destiny, cast to the pages of the *Akashic Record*— read but never known. I do not yet understand them.

*   *   *

We held hands. Looked deep into each other's eyes. Slowly, hers closed. She leaned forward and kissed my lips.

My eyes, they wanted to close, but they would not. Too much love to see, I did not want to lose a moment of it.

Chapter 6

On the train, into the dream or a nightmare. Post a traditional wait in a mass of Asian people going somewhere to nowhere mighty fast. My seat, window seat. An apparent business man, of sorts, over to my left side. I hoped he didn't want to talk to me. How shall I say it, I was not in the mood.

The train moved out. I watched the city change to scenery; the green of vegetation, painted onto a landscape, like an artist paying homage to a holy (wholly) canvas with brush in hand. The gray sky, distant, longing, gone to somewhere, nowhere—who knows where.

The guy next to me, he ate chicken—sold by a local girl who passed in the isles on the fringes of destiny. He was done, he reached over me, placed the remains into the plastic see through garbage bag that clung on the train's wall, beneath the window—by my closest to the window seat. *'Thanks a lot dude.'* Fuck!

A few hours out, a transfer of the train. I got up. The businessman and his eating remains, gone.

As I stood in the train station, I realized that it felt good to once again be *China Deep*. Lost in the extremities of Asia. Living life on the hard road.

Aboard a new train, no one sat next to me. It rolled on into the night. Nothing much to say, nothing much to do. Live as the moments of life pass by. Time, it continues on, far too fast. Leading to the door of the great abyss.

*   *   *

Time, like when I want to create something. Like when I want to know something. I want the barren time to mean more than zero. What does that time mean? In between the space where imagination meets reality and destiny is lost into the mortal wind.

Life, it is art. Live art and your each movement will be art. The ticking hands of time they are so cruel and unforgiving. When you are young, you have forever but as each moment comes then goes, age comes upon us all, with its knowledge that forever will only last until tomorrow and today will turn far too fast onto the next calendar page.

Is the wind ever really born? Does the wind ever really die?

*   *   *

AM next. I pulled into the appropriate station. I wondered if I was going to be met by Bloom. I wondered if I would have to stagger my way to some unknown *Secret Agent Man* location and find out finally like, *'What the fuck I was doing there?'*

Off the train. An old station, nothing much to describe. I mean after all, like this isn't a travel guide. It was a yellowish color; the walls that is; painted dark yellow. There was some of the basic government sponsored employees and a lot of locals pumping the environment full of *Shanghai-wa* dialect. The skin colors seemed to be fading to a golden hue, lighter than the tone prominent in HK—for whatever that is worth. I seemed to be the only white boy in the zone.

I made my movement forward, as movement always seems to be: the river, the flow, the time. I looked for the direction—headed for the front door.

I watched as eyes found their way onto me. Like I said, I was the only white boy.

Outside, I figured I was going to have to grab a taxi or something. *'Fuck that asshole, Bloom,'* I thought. *'Couldn't even get off his fat ass to come and get me.'*

I made it outside and was looking for a taxi. I had the basic dudes coming up to me as I exited the door trying to take me for a ride, Asian style. *"Oh good taxi, you come with me."* Fuck that, for if you know Asia, you know there are those taxis and then there are the real taxis. Where were the real taxis?

I was looking. As I was looking, digging for the native language address which had accompanied me from my civilized realms of civilization. You know the place, where they have the civilized mentality to plot to secretly change history, kill people, overthrow governments, and all of that kind of shit, just because things *ain't-a-go'n* their way.

Anyway, I felt a hand grabbed my arm. I was about to spin around and take somebody out

"Dr. Storm, I'm here to pick you up."

It was some local dude.

"Mr. Bloom has sent me."

Well, as previously alluded to, I'm not really a trusting person by nature, but it all seemed to be in the flow, so I let him lead on. He wanted to carry my bag. I thought I better just hang tough onto it, just in case...

We went to his car. It was actually a taxi that some young boy had been apparently watching for him. He threw the boy a couple crumbled up bills. He opened the door to the back seat. I planned to ride shotgun, but, AOK with me. I got in. We drove off.

"Where's Bloom," I inquired.
"We must pick him up."

There was some basic zero small talk spoken. Nothing worth writing about. I went for the cruise. The city was pumping with massive people. Like all of Asia seems to do.

*   *   *

The sky was cloudy. A cloudy gray. I liked it. It looked like mysticism. You know, like deep and distant. Like it had been cast in a spell by some sort of ancient mystic. I always liked it cloudy.

The buildings looked old, though some rose into the sky. Colors of brown, yellow—fading, blending into the stone carved essence of a forbidden past, surround by the concrete world.

We pulled up in front of one said building. Bloom was out in front. He saw our approach. He moved forward. He got in.

I could tell we already understood one another. I could feel his vibes. He sat down next to me in the rear seat. No longer did he extend his hand. An enemy; *'Good.'* At least we have a definition.

"Have a good train ride Samuel?"
"Why did you get to fly here?"
"Your entrance needed to occur less noticed. The airport is monitored."

Well, that sounded logical enough.

"So, what are we up to Jeff?"
"I will explain that and everything else to you when we get back to my house."

I could see the driver looking in the rearview mirror, studying our words and our actions.

"Who's he," I inquired.
"He works for us. But, that's not important."

Yeah, whatever. I just looked on out the window. I was in none too pretty of a mood. Basically, I was just in a *'Fuck you'* state of mind. If that asshole Bloom thought that he was going to be the one to give me orders, he was dreaming on the serious side. I chilled back though, witnessing life go by.

We pulled down a semi paved, semi dirt road, residential area; concrete houses, people out in front, people brushing their teeth, spitting into the street, clothing hanging to dry, people walking, a lot of people walking.

Up in front,

"Here we are."

A house like all the others, stone, plaster. A corner dwelling, nothing to brag about. We get out.

"Like, don't you have an office or something?"
"This is my office."

The driver drove off.

"He's not going to stay," I ask.
"This mission has nothing to do with him."
"Exactly what is this mission?"
"When we get inside..."

Old Bloom was trying to pull all his *macho* forward. *'I'm so fucking impressed,'* I thought. We walked through the door.

*   *   *

Sometimes destiny's hit is way too hard. You never see it coming. Sometimes you are given all that you ever wanted and you never even asked for it. Sometimes...

We go into the house. Through the door, like through the door of divine intervention. We are instantaneously greeted by a lady, and I don't use that word lightly. She was kill. I mean she was non-stop on: long black hair, piercing Chinese eyes, cheekbones to the sky; tall, for a girl from the PRC, maybe 5'7." ...Wore a pure white long dress, casual on the casual side of elegance. Our eyes met—my fate was sealed.

"Hello," she said in English. I could hear the accent in her voice.
"Hello," I answered.

Her name was... Well, I guess I shouldn't give her real name either. What should I call her? I don't know, I'll call her Ming-zhou.

Another dude came up to greet our arrival. Believe me, not so interesting as the aforementioned lady of dreams. He was another local, on the short side; maybe five-five—rather long in the forehead, if you catch my meaning—balding more than a bit. He wore a yellow polo style shirt, khaki brown, rather baggy, pants, and a lighter brown casual jacket. He stuck out his hand. His I shook.

Eyes and minds in motion. But me, I really couldn't give a flying fuck about anything other than this lady who had entered my field of vision. Entered and exited before my eyes had a chance to worship her heavenly form. The dude, the local, and her, gave their farewells and booked.

"Well Samuel, lets get down to business."
"What about them, aren't they a part of this?"
"Yes, but they've already been briefed. They just needed to meet you. They're here all the time and well prepared for what we're about to set out to accomplish."
"What about that babe, is she latched up with that guy?"
"Believe me Samuel, I know what's going through your mind. The same thing went through mine. You know I'm a man too." He hastens to add. *"But she is very locally orientated. You know how these people are."*

What an idiot...

"Yeah, but are they latched up?"
"No, they aren't involved. But, it would better for you to keep your mind on what you've been brought here to accomplish. Don't look at every woman as an object and you will find, as I have, life will go along much more smoothly."

Yeah right, fuck that! I mean we're all objects on this planet—in one form or another—like a bunch of fucking ants in an ant farm. We just think that we're doing something important. Me, give me the dream anytime. I mean like, a momentary dream is all that life adds up to anyway.

* * *

So, anyway back to the story at hand. Bloom, leads me to the other room of his two-room crib. His bed was in there, as well. I'm thinking he better not try to get fruity—bed in an office...

His crib was just one of your basic places. I guess since I'm telling the story here and all, I should try to describe the place a bit better for you. The walls, well, you could see the stone bricks. There was no interior wall. Great insulation, huh? A window here or there. A painting or three on the walls. Like you know the kind—real shit, swap meet art. And oh yeah, a picture of our president. Well, fuck him and fuck that. He had a wooden desk. His single bed and night stand over to the side. And, that be about that. Enough description for you?

"Like where's your telephone, fax, and your computer" I ask.
"I don't have them here. I use the one's at the big hotel. The local people don't have them and I wouldn't want to attract attention to myself."
"Attention to yourself... You're a fucking white guy living in the middle of a PRC ghetto!"
"Well, all the people know that I'm here but they believe me to be an architect helping to develop the housing in this district. That's my cover."
"Fucking great! Appearing to help the people, when you're... Just what the fuck are you doing here?"

So, a long story made short, again, he was just doing what he was doing. Like you know, all of the self-righteous politicians who manipulate the world and you never hear a word about it.

Bloom pulls out a map, chucks out some papers, and gives me my directions. Simple enough thing, or should I say *'thΛng.'*

The problem, the situation being, there was this almost superpower of a country, names shall remain nameless, though I suppose they are obvious. They were doing the old creating of—the chemical warfare within the bounds of said country—out in the outback. They were then selling said chemical weapons to another lower power, desiring superpower status, or at least the destruction of any populous deemed worthy of waging a *Jihad,* a holy war, against.

My job, *'Should I decide to accept it, Mr. Phealps,'* was to... Well, actually I guess I had no choice in acceptance or not at this point—my gig was to attempt to put 'em out-a-business: two locations, two jobs. Winner takes all. The loser, well the loser, he would probably be dead. Overall, seemed like a fair enough cause...

"What? Now! I just fucking got here and I am way too fucking tired!"
"Look Samuel, history does not wait for individual needs."

Fuck, I was on my way to the airport having been briefed; having been equipped. Briefed with virtual zero. Equipped with nothing but the promise I was to meet Yang-qui at the airport. Yang-qui, the local dude who left with Ming-zhou. But once there, the airport, I could not speak with him. In fact, I was not to speak to him even upon our arrival—just to follow him. He and I were to then contact some other homeboy locals on the town on the far side of midnight.

You know, like I don't want to sound unpatriotic here. For you know, really, I am. It's just that have you ever had that overwhelming feeling, like, *'What the fuck did I get myself into?'* Like, *'The avalanche is falling and I just walked right in front of it!'*

Anyway, on to the continuation of the journey...

The travel to this distant sight certainly did not bother me. I had been there before. But once there, I was dealing with full-blown reality. Something I hadn't had to face yet on this journey. I don't know, I guess it's kind of hard to explain— you know, fear.

Fear, it's an abstract feeling; a sensation. I came to know far too well in my years as a street kid growing up in the gang-ridden underside of L.A. Fear, like you're never quite sure where the next blow may come from or who may unleash it. Like, where I came up, you saw people getting *stived* or shot all the time, so you always had to be on your guard. Who was your friend today, sure the fuck wasn't going to be your friend tomorrow—you always had to be ready. I remember this one time, like my so-called best-friend came knocking at my door in the PM, asked me to come out, *"Sure."* As soon as I get out, I get jacked by like fifteen dudes. All because somebody said I said something I didn't say to someone who didn't like the sound of it. You got to watch your own back out there on the outside.

50

But fear, you just learn to live through it and walk on...

Anyway, no one else can feel your emotions but you. They mean nothing to anyone else. So, I won't bore you any further with mine. What do they prove anyway—they're here and then they're gone—like life...

On the road, I decide then and there, that this was my baby. Yeah, I would do the job as best I could: God and Country and all... But, I wasn't going to trust anyone or expect anything from anybody.

*   *   *

The airport, it was one of those crowded PRC scenes. Plastered white walls, plastered with people—all eyes on me, the white boy in the crowd.

I knew the airport, I had been through it once or twice before. I did the basic stand in line, get my seat assignment.

I didn't notice Yang-qui, though I, oh so casually looked. You know, playing my newly assigned *Secret Agent Man* roll and all. So, post the stand in line, post the call for the flight, post the through the security check, I was in the waiting area. Had me a tea. Would have preferred a brew, but no-go on that side of the picture.

It was boarding time—I boarded. A bit concerned as to the lack of the presence of my *compadre* but on I got. As I was isle seated and awaiting take off, there he passed me. He had to know I was there. It had to have been set up this way. But, he didn't even look. Almost too obvious, I thought, for all the other locals, sure filled their Asian eyes with my form. Like hey, take a picture, it lasts longer. But, if I had said that, they probably would have.

Chapter 7

And, the waves of her body caressed me, like the surf in the Asian sun. And, the dreams they seemed all to be answered. A kiss a touch, it was all mine.

I looked out around us as we lay on the beach in each other's arms. The blue of the sky, like a cold knife in the heart, as the sand in the minor vegetation, in which we lay, merged with her black hair.

I was next to her, but too far from her. The country, the culture, her programming—she desired to leave her clothing on. I was inside of her, my soul grasped in her body. The sky, the scene, it was all too perfect—everything I had ever wanted, more than I have ever deserved. Inside of her, but I was separate, the act, it was not whole.

"I love you Samuel," she said.

She didn't need to mention it as I already knew.

My mind drifted as our bodies moved in rhythm, *'What was to come of this? What was to come of her? Her and I—this land, this country?'* Thoughts stole my perfect moment. I could not control them. I wanted it all. I wanted this beach, this scene, this moment, this feeling, this serenity. I wanted my body inside of hers, forever... Forever and ever and ever…

Chapter 8

Off the airplane, the masses moved to nowhere—nowhere fast. I waited for Yang-qui to pass me. Then, I oh so coolly, casually, followed. It was a funny feeling. A feeling of like being in a daze. This journey, this adventure had come over me fast.   Yes, very fast.

There was no place to move in or out of the massive people. Like being one of the dominos standing straight, as the row was pushed, and they all tumbled to the ground. It's like, have you ever unconsciously stared at the sun while your mind was wondering somewhere else. Maybe it's for a minute, maybe it's five, but then you realize that you were staring at the sun, but it's too late, your eyes are forever scarred and you have confirmed that your thoughts can damn you, take you away from your currently reality into a place that never really existed.

I moved on, pushed by the masses—too far, too slow. Off the plane into the airport, I followed at a distance behind Yang-qui. All eyes were on me, none were on him. The thought, the wonder came to me, *'Why did they choose a guy like me, who sticks out in this Asian crowd like I do?'* But I moved on.

Out to the outside, Yang-qui moved. I saw him look, as if wondering where to go. Then he moved to the left, walking to the side of the airport. This one, this airport, was larger than the previous; newer by the standards of history. For literary sake: gray cement, plastered with stone along its base. Its control tower rose high—high as far as PRC buildings go. Rose to the sky, tall, gray, and wide—as the heavens above shadowed down their grayness, hiding the blue. I could feel it; a storm was to come.

I was noticed, but not really asked as to my destination. No one asked if I needed a taxi. These local, they didn't seem to care. On to the side of the building—first Yang-qui turned, I followed. And, for an instant I wondered, *'Would he be there when I circled the corner or killed by a bullet in the head?'*

A black, red roofed, car awaited. Taxi, it said. Yang-qui had already gotten into the front seat, passenger side. He reached around, opened the rear door for me to ride in the back seat. I got in. We drove off.

The city, this city, was maybe twenty minutes or half an hour from the airport. Yeah, I had cruised in here before; two years the previous. It was a city necessarily *en route* to one of the most sacred places on the Earth, the heart of the Himalayas—occupied;   names   shall   remain nameless.

*   *   *

Since then, since that point, since that two years the previous, all the places I had traveled to, all the things I had done, were just based in the fulfillment of momentary desires. For once you encounter the source of mysticism, and like a fool, turn away from it, nothing else ever really matters, you know that you are damned. Thus, there I was, doing this...

As we motored towards the city, the landscape was more covered with vegetation then most regions of the PRC. There were crops, cows, even a dog or three, running wild. The people were agriculturally based; carrying things on their backs, on their heads, on two ends of a stick across their shoulders. Anyway, enough of the demographics, I'm not doing a cultural study. I was there for WAR.

We didn't talk much as we drove. The driver, tall, rather dark, rather dirty; bushy hair, wearing a plaid shirt. He and Yang-qui, they spoke, but I could tell, feel, their conversation was strained.

We pulled into the town, maybe twenty minutes deep. Dusk was falling and the wide main thoroughfare was lined with bicycles, ox carts, and, yes, even a few motorcars—very few.

We eventually veered to the left and cruised on down this minor, semi dirt road. Houses and businesses lined it. We passed an open-air pool hall; front doors open wide: three tables. I thought to go in and shoot myself a game or two, like I do with the boys down on the row—skid row, back L.A. But no—no time for games, this was the real world: obligations, commitments, and a lot of things I knew nothing about. I could sure have used a cold one though. This place did have one mean, local brew, green tea leave beer. I remembered...

Not far, to the left again, a smaller road, to a house; plastered white, fading gray to brown. It was almost dark: time, life, and destiny were at hand.

We pulled up, got out, the taxi it drove off. The crib just slightly removed enough to not draw attention to the fact of a white boy making his way inside.

Inside, it was dim, white-walled. We were alone. Yang-qui suggested I sit down. I did. Did I want some tea? *'Negatory, dude.'*

He sat down to discuss our plan and reveal to me much more then I had known before about what we were set out to do. He spoke directly, no bullshit going on here. I liked it. No time to play games. He, Yang-qui, was this serious no nonsense sort of dude.

'*Bam,*' in walks the taxi driver. I jumped up like a *mutha' fucker*. I was about to kick some ass. …Had my small canvas bag of a suitcase in hand to chuck it in the face of the dude as a diversion. He jumped back. But, all unnecessary action, based in adrenal rush and not near enough sleep—at least not enough sleep on my part.

Anyway, post a brief laugh at the situation, and the completion of the prepatory *convo,* Yang-qui suggested that I go and get some sleep for we would be full on at 3:00 in the A of M. He showed me to a small room. There was a bed, no sleets. A towel lay over the mattress, a towel over the pillow. I smiled to myself. Last time I was in this town, on my way to *Holy-ville,* I slept in a hotel that had provided me with exactly the same accommodations.

Yang-qui closed the door behind him. Left me alone in the alone. Alone, it actually made me a bit paranoid. Like, just what was he up to.

I walked the room. The windows were boarded up. AOK. I tired the door handle. The door; no lock. AOK. I looked for a quick, if necessary, weapon of self-defense. The only thing I came up with was a support piece from the rear of a wooden chair. It was loose. I pulled it out. Kept it in hand.

As I begun to lie down, I realized that I needed to hit the head, drain the old lizard. But like hey, there was no connecting bathroom to the master suite so I just chilled back. Had to hold it.

I kicked back, stared at the cracking, falling plaster and light orange paint that made up the darkness. The night was hot, humid, stuffy, and there was no ventilation or fan. It's very hard for me to sleep in said situations. It is like sometimes that kind of heat forces me to awaken, like first my mind comes alive, while my body remains lost in the realms of the paralysis of REM sleep. That's like hell. I have to use all of my mental strength to try to shake this part of my body or that part of it to wake up. Sometimes I can, sometimes I can't. As I lay there, I thought back, to how, as an adolescent, that feeling used to haunt me, until I isolated its cause and then had the ventilation full on. But, here now, *nada* I could do about it.

I began to doze off, realizing how little sleep I had actually gotten in the past few days. Hell, it was just a week or so ago that I got an AM phone call setting all this into motion.

I lay there reflected how I'm such a light sleeper and I checked the atmosphere for noise. There was none. No doubt due to our semi removed location and the fact that Yang-qui and the driver must be laid back too. AOK with me, I thought. I fell into sleep. I thought how Siam would way have to be a far better place to be right now, chilling down the evening with some babe of passion. I thought, yeah, I thought... I went to sleep.

*   *   *

I felt a hand on my shoulder. I jumped, about to pop the punk with the pseudo club I still had in my hand.

They jumped back. I jumped up. I was still in my clothing, of course.

But, I did not need to swing. My eyes, my vision, I was embraced by a waking vision of the goddess. Yes, I had come to know her. I had seen her before: Thailand, Tibet, Nehon.

But, I was shocked/surprised; I didn't even know that she was a part of this. I did not even expect her to show. But, there she was, this human form of the divine. The one I have given the name of Ming-zhou.

She was here. I was there. In the darkness, I would have just preferred to have loved her. Loved her until she could take no more.

Me, I was still in the dream state. I wished, knew then—hoped that this dream state could last forever. Me, her, the dark, the night, the love.

"Mr. Storm, be careful, you may hurt yourself," she exclaimed.

Hurt myself… I already had done that a long time ago. This was just one more act in my theatre of destruction.

"Get ready Mr. Storm. We must be on our way," Yang-qui voiced those words from the semi kinda hallway, outside my door.

I looked at myself. I guess I was ready, for I had slept in my clothes. I grabbed by bag.

"Should I take this with me," I asked.
"Yes, we probably won't be coming back here."

I didn't like the sound of that. Just what did he mean? But before much thinking could go into it, all of us were in the car. We were on the road.

59

Ming-zhou, Yang-qui, and I riding in the back seat. The driver, front, he drove on.

I was spaced, distant—again way wondering why, how, I had ended up doing such a thing. All this while the leg of Ming-zhou rested, oh so gently, against mine.

There was no real talking going down. I felt my palms; they sweated as we drove through the deserted side streets of this, deep in the heart of central China, city.

I stuck my hands in my olive colored shirt's front pocket to check to see if I had my sun glasses and to casually, coolly, hoping it would go unnoticed, dry my hands off on the outside of my shirt. It was dark you know. . .

I reached in my pocket. I pulled out this little winged pin of a piece of jewelry they had laid on me upon the air flight. I looked at it. Ming-zhou looked at me looking.

"Did you have a good flight Mr. Storm," she inquires.
"So-so. And please, just call me Spencer. Here, you want this?"

She accepted it, like it was the greatest gift she had ever been given. Maybe it was. I don't know?

"Oh thank you Mr. Storm. Oh, I mean Spencer."

Like where was my head, a full-on babe was sitting next to me. And me, I was in full-on paranoia. *'You have to take a few deep breaths there, big guy,'* I thought to myself.

The way we went through the city took some time. More time than it should have taken—the side streets and all. No attention needed, none called for. It was a dark and eerie drive, almost surreal. As we passed old building that appeared almost colonial, others that were nothing more than cardboard shacks. And, I had the divine goddess sitting next to me...

Chapter 9

And in the moment of love, the passion of embrace, there can be nothing more. As my body had entered her body—as I was inside of her. As her embrace had wrapped itself so tightly around me, I knew that there could be nothing else that would even come close to mattering. Was this what I had been looking for all of this time? Looking, dancing, destroying myself in the process. And then, finally becoming far too tainted to not even care anymore, just saying, *"Fuck it,"* it does not exist.

Or, was this just another one of those momentary nothing infatuations: love lived, love lost, love lived again. Yeah, for I had been through those once or three hundred times before.

And, who had she known before. Where else had her body been?

She kissed me on my neck. I looked into her eyes. The thousand things that the mind can do to rob you of the moment. I had almost forgotten how little anything else but this feeling of enormity matters, for however long that it may last.

Chapter 10

Outside of the town, we continued along what seemed to be a side road. Oh yes, did I mention the headlights still remained in the off position—had the entire journey. There was little conversation going down. Maybe I was the only one that was chill factor zero about the whole prospect of the impending doom of this mission.

There was no doubt at what was to be accomplished. Who was to do what, when or why. It was detailed, by Bloom, by Yang. Yang, who was actually a far better detailer and far more humble in the process of said details then the semi self-righteous Bloom.

For me, the problem was, it was all abstract: the location, the setting, the etcetera. The rest of them had no doubt viewed the situation before, first-hand. It was me who was out in the cold.

Down the road we went, there in the distance I saw lights reflecting against the clouds of the nighttime sky. The thought passed in my mind of how perfect the colors shaped themselves against the gray and blue of the night. Then my mind went to the art of it all and like yeah, why hadn't I ever been able to do life, live life, that-a-way, in my art. Instead, here I was playing James Bond with a lot less cool and a lot fewer babes.

A lot of thoughts of nothing go through your mind in a life unfulfilled. It's kind of funny, you know. I sit here now writing about my experiences; things are always better in memory, I guess. Or, is it just my lack of ability to be in the now, as it were. The mind, it takes you a million places to nowhere.

It was like an Asian Christmas tree, as we pulled closer into full view. A power plant— massive industrialization that fully sparkled, as chimneys that rose to the sky spit out pollution and gasses, in a country where there was not yet any need for control.

It was almost scary, fear placed in the palm of your hand. For my destiny lay here. Now, was no longer a question, for now was now.

We were maybe four or five hundred yards from the outside, fenced wall of the factory. Semi hidden, semi deep in what minor tree lined vegetation there was on the outskirts of the plants lifeline. Post that, the vegetation had all been cleared. It made room for an awesome structure, in a land that had not yet reached this level of automation.

Grasses surround it. In the reflective glow of the orange and yellow white lights, I could see that by day these grasses would be green, would be yellow.

Just how the fuck was I supposed to make it from here to there without being noticed!

Though there were no searchlights, like in all the movies, no armed men patrolling in tanks, a movement forward would have to been noticed. I mean nobody is about to have this kind of shit going on without some kind of surveillance, you know.

The car stopped. We got out. I to the right, Yang to the left. Ming-zhou, well, she slides it on, out my side. Good sign, I thought.

Yang went for the trunk, before any words of discussion could really be spoken. He pulled out what looked to be three gray grease monkey suits. You know the kind, like the one-piece jumpsuits, the kind like they wear at the Indy 500. He hands one my direction,

"You better put this on, so you don't get your clothes dirty."

I took it. But like, why?

He hands one in Ming-zhou's direction, as well. She begins to put it on. And, he chills on with his.

"What's going on? Like why do we need these?"
"Because the way you are getting into the plant is a tunnel which we dug months ago."
"Months ago? Why months ago?"
"Because we wanted to be sure that it was not discovered."
"Yeah, but how do you know that it is even still there?"
"It is. We've checked it."

Now, this thought was setting none too well with me. In fact, the more I thought about it, none of this whole fucking situation was setting well with me.

"Why didn't you tell me this, man? You guys have been keeping me in the fucking dark about everything!"
"That isn't our intention, Mr. Storm. We just all have our individual assignment to accomplish. And the less one knows about the others, and the less

unnecessary knowledge one has about their own, the easier the mission is accomplished."
"Yeah, right..."

I thought that was a bunch of fucking bullshit but there wasn't much that I could do about it. Aside from looking like a pussy and bailing from the whole thing all together. And, with a babe in the presence, that was way no-go.

"Now, Mr. Storm..."
"Just call me S."
"Okay, S. When you return from inside you will take this motorcycle."

At which point he walks over by this tree a few feet away and lifts a netted and camouflaged cover off of this little two wheels of a scoot. Well, fuck me...

"Once you have accomplished your goal you will come back here, get this motorcycle, and ride it back into town. It will be daylight by then, so be sure to wear the helmet to hide your blonde hair. Ride it a few blocks from Hotel X."

...Names remaining nameless and all. In fact, once upon a time, I even stayed at Hotel X. Back in the day...

"From there, walk to the hotel and catch a taxi to the airport. If all goes according to plan you will be there just in time to catch this flight."

With that he hands me an air ticket.

"What about you? Where will you be?"
"I will be there too. But under no circumstance make contact with me."
"AOK. What about her?"
"She will be returning a bit later."

So anyway, long stories made short and all... He leans the scoot up against a tree. And gives the, *"Let's go."*

A few feet away, the other direction, Yang moves this dirt, lifts this cover and, yeah, there was a tunnel down there.

I mean, I was none too happy about this *sit-e-ation* at all. It did not look to stable, if you catch my meaning. I mean, fuck, it was like straight out of some old movie, you know. But flash light in hand; in he drops, followed by Ming-zhou. Well, double fuck me again. In I go too.

I mean here we were sliding through this dirt. The tunnel was wide enough to crouch over in and kinda walk. Easier for them, as they were way shorter than me. It kind of reminded me of the walk up the inside to the inner chamber in the Great Pyramid in Egypt. I mean like, I knew that my back and my legs were going to be way sore from walking this way.

And then, the thought comes to me of how they had dug this tunnel a few months back. And, maybe like, the security of the factory was just like fully waiting for someone to actually use it before they blew it up on their heads or something like that. This was not glamorous.

The tunnel went on for a-ways. It was fucking gross. I could not help but think that there must be bugs, snakes, and rats all around me. Yang had the flashlight. I did not. He was several feet in front of me, so maybe he was seeing that shit and I was not. Well, better him then me, I guess.

We get up ahead a bit and it is stop.

"Right up there S. You can see it."

Yang flashes his light that direction.

"That's where this tunnel exits into the large ventilation system. From there Ming-zhou will lead you."
"Woe dude, I ride this road alone. I don't want the responsibility of anybody else."

Ming-zhou standing there, well kinda standing as she couldn't really fully stand up; looking all the way bummed and stuff.

"Look S, she is a trained operative. She knows what she is doing. She can speak the language far better then you and she has been inside the complex many times and knows exactly where to take you. This matter is not open for discussion. She's going!"

Well, he put me in my place. Fuck him.

Now, I never have been one to take orders very well. And his words, (again), brought up the feeling that I pretty much had continually since I had started out on this adventure, that I should just say, *'Fuck it'* and leave. But in too deep, like deep under the ground you know. So, what could I do? I would just have tap up this *mutha' fucker* for talking to me in such an authoritarian tone later but, for now, I guess, I would just have to live it.

He pulls a flash light from his pocket,

"Here use this when you go back."

Thanks, a whole fucking lot for not giving it to me on our way through the tunnel, dude.

"I'm leaving now. Good luck S."

He lays the same rap on Ming-zhou, in their native tongue. He slides on by and it's *gones-ville Daddy-0,* down the snake hole.

I kind of look at Ming-zhou for a moment or ten. Like one of those stare deeply into the depths of the eyes; love forever—like when you know it/realize it and all. But, time to move...

There was a bit of more light down at the end of the tunnel. I proceeded. She followed. We reached the opening.

Chapter 11

As I stare into her eyes, as I embrace her, Ming-zhou. The waves moved behind us. The sun sheds it warm presence, letting us know that it contains the essence of the absolute. I held her. I knew her. Now, I have had her. Now, she has had me.

There was no conquest. Though no doubt the feeling and thought of said did race through my mind initially, at least for a bit. Somehow, more than that, I almost felt a loss. A loss of the known innocence. I guess that is something I have never known; innocence.

But her, as she lay in my arms, as I was inside of her, as just the slightest amount of sweat found its way into my clothing, making my shirt form closely to me. Like a protective shell, like a shield—protection for my heart. And we were together, we had kissed, we had touched. And though the overwhelming feeling of love over took me, I knew that her embrace would never be distant, never be a fantasy again. For now, it had been felt, known. And, as the first kiss is the only kiss, the only one that ever really matters. For it can never be known, never be felt again.

The thinking mind loses its innocence. Techniques may be developed, intimacy may come, but the first is the last once it is lost forever. May I learn to travel through the realms of time, so it may once again be felt.

I looked in her eyes. I closed mine, kissed her. I tried to escape the inevitable that every kiss hello, equals a sad tear of goodbye.

Chapter 12

The ventilation tunnel was not as big as yang had led me to believe it would be. It was about the same size as the snake hole, just metal platted. I stared down it as we pushed a cut piece of metal to one side. I sliced my hand a bit as we did. *"Fuck!"*

"We should take these suits off here S."

As we were removing our *gear-head* jump suits, the thought did come to my mind as hers was being unzipped. Well... You know... Instead, I inquire.

"Where are we going exactly, Ming-zhou?"
"I will show you."
"Why don't you just tell me and wait here."

Unsuited, she walked on, down the tube.

She said, *"We don't have time to discuss it."*

*   *   *

Me, I don't like being closed in—call it claustrophobia if you will. I don't think anyone really does. But we hunched our way on and down the shaft, as I followed her.

There was a bit of water in the base of the ventilation shaft and I just knew there had to be rats and those giant fucking big Asian cockroaches in there. And hey, this was a chemical plant. Man, I just knew I was walking in some deadly fucking chemical shit. What was this going to do to me? Really fuck me up? I knew it! I mean like I just really way far knew it! Like I was probably not going to be able to have babies and stuff. Well, who cares about that, anyway—don't want any...

As we neared our designated end, Ming-zhou, with finger to her lips, gave me the old chill and be silent sign. She held the other hand up, telling me to like, *"Wait."* She walked up and turned this corner. I couldn't see her for a moment. A feeling that I did not like.

Amazing how a million years of reality can be lived in only a few short seconds.

She reemerged around the corner and gave me the, *"Come on."* I followed like a whipped little puppy dog.

Around the corner there were voices. She halted me again. I could hear them walk by as they spoke the dialect of... Well, no. I can't say. You know, national security and all. But, it was not a native indigenous dialect.

As she turned around she looked at me, reached to the back of her hair, removed a hair barrette, and handed it to me. Motioned that I should put it in. I smiled, I did. Then she motioned that I should tuck my hair down inside my collar. *"Yes, masta."* I obliged.

The voices passed. She led me down on my knees, through an even smaller tunnel which entered into what looked to be a ventilation shaft, that exited through a large thick round metal door, which she peered through, oh so consciously, and then exited into a hall. I followed. We were fully upright. The first time, in well, how shall I say, a long time.

We were inside the plant.

You know, I kind of expected a way massively modern facility. Like a hospital, like in the movies. But it was cold, old: concrete and plaster. Gray, in color. With a little white painted here and there.

Expectations… I guess that taught me an essential lesson right there.

We walked on. She said no words to me. She was in front. I tried to come up next to her but with a gentle sweeping motion of her arm she just guided me back a bit. We passed a clipboard hanging on a wall. She grabbed it. Carried it as if she was looking/reading it. Like, what fucking game is going on here? Like, let's get this shit over with and bail. I mean my heart, needless to say, was a-full on pumping. Me, I did a few deep breaths hoping to cool it down.

There were people up ahead, all of them Caucasoid racial stock. She glanced back at me. We walked on. We passed to little notice. I nodded to this one dude who caught my glance.

Now, finally… I understood why they had brought me here—wanted a honky in tow. *Quai low* in the Cantonese tongue: ghost eyes.

They were all fucking white boys in this place. And, though I didn't rap their lingo, I suppose my eyes of blue fit in a wee bit better then would Asian eyes.

Down a hall here, up the stairs there. I walked on, cool and *non-cha-lant*. We passed others—white boys, except for a local, sitting in an office, secretary or three. All were clad in way casual clothing. Though I prefer wearing a sport coat, I guess these people knew their business and the threads they had set me up with were AOK.

I could not help but wonder where we were walking. From the semi distant view of the plant I had from the outside, it looked all fairly well contained in a large singular structure. We walked on. My mind head-tripped on.

Up a gray stairwell, there was a door, painted white, housing a hazy window pane with some writing of a dude's name upon it. In, she goes. In, I follow.

There was a desk, office front. No one was sitting at it. Just the standard type of office: old wooden desk, file cabinets. A second door led on. I followed on. A man sitting rapidly gets up, looking at me, saying something. Ming-zhou moves right up to him. *'BAM,'* she knife-handed him right in the throat—like the perfect expert, positive expression.

He keels over his desk. I see the blood running from out of his mouth. This dude was way dead. Fuck, what was going on?

She moves to a picture, pulls it down. A safe was exposed. She goes right for the combination, opens it in just a few. Damn, where did she get that combo?

First, she grabs out some papers. Then, grabs a lighter from the man's desk. Dead men tell no tales... She fires the papers up and lets them burn in a trashcan. Then, she grabs a box, wooden, stained brown, and hands it to me. Out of the dress she is wearing, she pulls this kinda rectangular box with a metal casing. Black, it was black. She pushes a button, switch, or something on it and begins to walk out of the door. I kinda stood there looking. "Come on," she so calmly says. The first words she has spoken to me since we had gotten inside. Again. I follow her as she locks the dead dude's door upon leaving and we walk on back and into the series of halls.

Chapter 13

"Don't stop S. Nothing has ever felt this good, this perfect."

I translated this for you, as she spoke it in her native tongue.

I had not stopped, somehow I had simply faded to a dream somewhere, someway, where my mind had allow itself to believe that it was laying on a Asia beach making love to the most perfect of women. A dream...

A dream, but then every dream has the potential of becoming a nightmare. For all dreams hold only the same promise of eternity. The same vow of forever. Eternity, forever, what do they mean? They all end in so short of a time.

The Christians, the Buddhists, the Hindus, the religious, the holy in general, they dream up the greatest ways for us, for the *'I'* to go on forever— forever and ever. Great dream. Too bad that they are all fiction.

"What are you think about S.?"
"Oh, nothing. Just about how much I love you."
"I love you too."

There, I had said it. There, I had meant it. How many times have those words been spoken? How many times was it only a lie? How many times was it cast into the bounds of the temporary? How many times...

I looked into her eyes; the brown reflected the blue of the sky. I was still inside of her. I held her tight once again and began to put the moves back on.

Chapter 14

We were taking a different route this time. I did not take the time to question. We passed a person or three; a nod met a nod, here or there. A disinterested glance was met with the same.

And like a too full of the *love juice* high-heeled whore on a Saturday night, we made our way quickly and directly to some indeterminate location that I knew not where. The pace was calculated but precise. She, Ming-zhou, was a fine-tuned war machine. Me, I could feel the sweat running down my forehead.

We had gone a-ways, walking, walking. As we passed this one guy, kinda big burly type, way bigger then me: wore a gray shirt, brown pants—he said something to me. What? How the fuck should I know? I just smiled and nodded, tried to keep a walking. He said something more. I laughed, looked at Ming-zhou. She at me. We kept walking. The dude kinda jogs up, grabs my sleeve, stopped me, while he's *rap'n* something.

Ming-zhou says, *"Get him off of you."*

I look at him. I look at her. The moment of truth.

"Come on S!"

This was why I had been hired. . .

I changed the box, I had been carrying, from my right hand, which the dude is holding the sleeve of, to my left hand. I smile at him. Instantly, I swing my arm back around his holding arm, locking his elbow. Snap, no games. I break it… His elbow that is.

"Awh, Awh" The fucking guy starts screaming.

I realized my folly. *'You don't hurt 'em, you gotta really fuck 'em up.'*

"Awh, Awh," he keep screaming and yelling something to someone, I know not who.

Ming-zhou grabs my arm, pulls me, we start to run. I am still following her. We go up some stairs. I see people. This is way no-go… She keeps going, straight towards them. The *honkys* are yelling something. At me, I guess. The locals, a secretary or two, actually about five, sending the vibes Ming-zhou's direction, in their dialect. We come face-to-face.

Without even a thought she goes right for the first guy of the incoming barrage and *'BAP,'* take out his knees with her foot and gives him one of those sweet little knife hands to the throat. He goes down.

'Fuck,' I think. For a second it is all like in slow-motion. I am just witnessing what is going down. Somebody grabs Ming-zhou, a big guy, two arms from behind, and though she gives him a heat butt to the nose, which starts to bleed, he does not let go. One guy comes at me, I front kick him right under the jaw, which sends him flying.

I go straight for the guy who is holding her. She is twisting and turning. I come from behind, grab the back of his hair, pull is head straight back, while I am giving him a foot to the back of his knee.

This action releases his grip enough so Ming-zhou breaks free. She turns, gives him a base of the palm strike right under his nose, shoving the old nose cartilage right up and into his brain. Probably killed him. I do not know…

One of the secretaries had jumped on my back by this point. I shove back. I slammed her against the wall. Before I even had to turn around and decide whether I was going to have to jam her up, Ming-zhou had grabbed her by the back of the head, gave her a knee to the face and threw her into the wall.

The other lady who didn't seem interested in the fisticuffs, just stood there. Ming-zhou, right over to her, *'BAM'* another palm hand to the nose, she was down, she was out-a-there.

Ming-zhou yelled, *"Come on,"* and started to run. I followed expecting that we were heading for the tunnel, but no, I could feel it, this was not the same way we had come in.

We entered into a something like a boiler room where there were people walking and working in white coats. It was noisy, loud, with pressure being pushed everywhere. No one seemed to notice us. She told me to wait by the door. She went and placed another one of those rectangular shaped things under one of the piles that led to this big vat. *"Let's go!"*

She was the boss. She knew the scene. I was nobody. I followed.

We had gone down some stairs, two, maybe three; switchback set—entered a hall, *'Fuck me!'* About ten dudes coming our direction—appearing none too pleased.

It happened so fast, we were right in the middle of them. *'BAM,'* I gave the first guy a roundhouse punch to his nose—sent it to the other side of his face. The stupid fucker rushed right into it. Force meets force. He went down, but this was not going to finish it. I felt a fist meeting with the back of my head. I pivoted. I back kicked right into the sucker-punching fucker's knee. He screamed. With my free hand, the touch of death; for I too knew the knife hand across the throat. He went down, dead.

Ming-zhou was tying it up with three or four. But, most of the attention seemed to be on me. I needed distance. I needed space to fight. I needed both hands free.

I skipping side kicked my way through a dude. Pushed another one to the side. I got up against a wall. I set the box, well almost threw it, down. Now, I was pissed, my life was on the *mutha' fucking* line, and me, I was ready to dance.

First guy comes up, straight fist to his throat. My punching hand reached around him, I grabbed his hair, left hand grabbed his shoulder, I pivoted his body against his head. I heard the crack. Like a deadly chiropractor, that neck was out-a-there. I held him for a second that felt like an eternity. I felt his life force flow out of him. He went limp in my grasp.

No time! I threw him against an oncoming assailant, which pushed him back. Another coming from the side; I threw a side kick right to his face. He went back, I followed through with a skipping side kick, hard, full-on, to his guts. I heard bones break. He went down.

Now I was warmed up, primed, pumping, pure adrenalin. I was dancing. I was ready. I was on the move. Now they had to come to me.

Next one up, he was punching. I threw an in-to-out block. I reached around, locked up his arm. I held him in place. I shot a fist right to his nose. *'BAM,'* blood spurted everywhere. I hit him one time, two times, three times, then a knife hand right in the throat.

This was no fucking movie. This was real life. There was no time to be pretty. This was life or death—mine.

Next one up at the batter's mound, he was coming, coming fast. He was going to swing, I could see it, feel it, anticipate it, I jumped back, he swung through, his momentum kept him flying. As he went, I threw a roundhouse kick to his head. It hit him hard, I saw him stagger down.

They were still coming, two more. I could see 'em. No time to waste, no time to kill, especially not mine. Skipping sidekick, I threw it to his knee. I could feel my foot go through almost to the other side. Kick still in motion, I threw it to his face, then I grabbed his neck, again I twisted, pulled, it/he was gone.

One more, eye-to-eye. I almost felt like I wanted to dance, wanted to play with this one. The battle had already been won. I saw the fear in his eyes. He straight swung at me. I leaned back, front kicked him to the groin, front kicked him under the jaw. He went back, he was on the floor. I leaned over. I lifted his head from the ground. I punched him one time full-on, face central.

I felt free, accelerated, ON, as I looked at all those bad boys who lay dead around me. It felt like a long battle but the whole process was probably just this side of a minute.

Then I heard a skirmish. Ming-zhou! I had almost forgot... Everybody was down and out around her, everybody but one who had her in a headlock.

"Hey asshole," I yelled.

He didn't look, which pissed me off even more. I thought to cold cock him, but I didn't want to mess up and or maybe break my hand on his thick fucking head. So, I ran, more like it felt like I flew over there. Really there was no thought, it all just kinda like happened, you know. *'BAP,'* I gave him a full on shot to his semi flabby, partially over weight kidneys that were covered by a blue work shirt. He jerked but not enough to suit me.

He was draining the air from Ming-zhou. I could hear her gasp. And, as he was crouched over, almost on his knees, what was the best form of attack for this big bruiser. I jump back, a full *'BAP,'* I *wang-chunged* him right-square in the balls from the backside with a front kick. He released. I grabbed his hair, his face—twist—crack, and another one down, another broken neck.

By the time I had done that, Ming-zhou was already up. *'What a fucking warrior,'* I thought

"Where's the box, S!"
"Right over there."
"Get the box, let's go!"

Fucking box. What was it anyway?

I grabbed it. We ran. We got to the exit point with no more incidents. We were actually already very close to it—geographically speaking and all. Into the tube. *'Like, woe total maximum riding the curl, dude.'* She closed the entry point behind her. We sprinted down the tunnel. I didn't even think to

82

change into the grease monkey jumpsuit. I just grabbed the flashlight and kept on going.

Smash, I ran right into the wall at the end of the tunnel. Dazed, but I pushed my way forward and up I went into the light.

Yes, it was light now. It way daylight.

I looked: one second, two seconds, three seconds... Again, seeming eternity. But, then her head popped up from the hole. I helped her up. We went over to the bike. A bad little kick-start puppy, you know. It was up, it was on. We were *Gonesville-Daddy-O.*

As we drove on, full on, sailing on pure adrenaline. Man, the wind in my hair, on my face, even in my eyes, though it made them water, it felt kill. Though I wouldn't have used that word right then.

Ming-zhou was riding shotgun, holding on tight. I had the pedal to the metal, as it were, and we were going when, *'BAM'* I heard this major eruption, which shattered and shook the ground on which we rode. I looked around me. I looked behind me. I almost lost control of the bike, but the plant, it was way in flames.

The little rectangular boxes, no doubt...

Like, you know man; if you can't hide the evidence, destroy it.

We pulled into town; she gave me the basic *di-rect-i-on(s).* A couple of blocks from the hotel, we dumped the bike as planned. She walked one direction, I walked the other.

"Aren't you going with me?"
"No, I'll see you back in...." (Oh yeah, I can't say the city....)

I didn't really like it, but I just walked on in the early morning hours. I tried to relax, breathe deep, but that was way no-go, man. I mean like... Well, you know...

I got to the front of the hotel. In fact, I had stayed there once or twice. Didn't I already tell you that? Once upon a time of course...

There were a few hippies, Westerners of course, waiting for the *Cheap-o Econo* bus ride to the airport. There was a taxi waiting in front, as well. I just went up and got right in. Airport, I said in the native lingo.

The doorman, chills on up, and expresses his distaste at my just getting in for others had summoned it. I reached in my pocket, slipped him a local *fin*. We drove on through the city, down a country road. It all seemed way longer for some reason this time. It took hours and hours of forever to *never-never-land* but finally we got there.

I paid him. Got out. Went inside. I pulled out my ticket, checked the time on my timepiece. Yes, there was time. I looked around... Didn't expect to see Yang but I looked for him anyway...

I went, leaned up against a wall, not far from other Westerners. ...Apparently a tour group of one sort or another. You know, I did it, to blend in and all.

And yes, I noticed him. There across the room, he sat. Yang—eye contact.

He got up. He walked my direction. I watched his movements. I watched the entire scene awaiting another confrontation—not with him; just with whomever. Aware, I was way too aware.

He walked up next to me, leaned against the wall. He sat my small suitcase down. He pulled at his shirt a bit to let me know, *'Like hey, feel the energy. You are way dirty, man. You should clean up.'*

I hadn't even thought of it but when I looked down at my clothing, I was a dirty mess. Mud, dirt, blood. He motioned with his eyes the direction of the bathroom. I saw it. I held the wooden box out, which still remained in my possession to indicate that he may want it. He just gave a slight nod, *"No,"* and walked away.

I stood back for a while just to check down on the *sich.* Then, I waltzed on over to the bathroom to change up.

I went into a stall. I took the clothing off, reached in my bag and pulled on two of my three piece supplied wardrobe. I thought that I should probably keep the stuff and get it cleaned up, but then, *'No. Fuck it. They probably had chemicals all over them. And, for sure, they had the vibes of all those whose lives I had taken.'* So, I just trashed them. Leave them and the vibes for the next person down the line. I put the box in the newly created luggage space.

I walked back into the main hall. It was large inside this building. Upon arrival, I had somewhat side stepped it. Though my memories were rekindled as to its features once I was inside.

Grey, everything was grey around here/there. Even when it was painted white, it all looked grey. High ceiling, way high. Maybe a million feet high. I don't know. Some wooden benches. Some wooden windows to toss your luggage through. Some wooden counter tops to purchase your tickets over. And life, I saw it pass through my hands so quickly. What does it mean anyway?

*   *   *

The flight was called. I went to the line to pass through the checkpoint. Yang, this time, he stood close behind—about two people behind me. *Guardian Angel.* But, could he be trusted?

I stood there... It was all like coming down from *the beans* (speed) or coke. Like when you are way geared up; heart pumping fast, mind even faster, and you gotta come down, sooner and later, and you way sure do not want to. Like, I was so *hyped* and I just wanted to get the fuck out-a-Dodge.

Maybe I was shaking a little bit, I don't know. Sweating, yeah. I knew that I was doing that. I looked at my ticket; it was wet in the palm of my hand. I looked; I even had a boarding pass. I hadn't realized it—hadn't even thought about it. I hadn't even checked in. How the fuck did Yang pull that one off. Well, I guess that bad dude had his ways...

I looked behind me, over my shoulder; it was almost like an instinctive type of feeling. I looked. Yang's head was turned, as well.

Through the door, large and almost colonial, walked one, no two men. Caucasian men. Two men, I knew where they were a-coming from. With them, with the two *quai-lo* or *la-ways* (in the Mandarin tongue; as you prefer), were two uniformed police officers. They walked, their eyes were opened.

Yang's head turned back my direction, as if to get my attention. Eye-to-eye our glances met. He motioned to leave the line, follow him. As nonchalantly as possible, I would leave.

First, I looked at my watch, then at the clock upon the wall. Not to attract any attention to myself, I looked around a bit at the very long line of

86

predominantly locals that had formed. Like, you know dude, *'Locals only.'* Then, casually I left the line, threw a smile the direction of the tourists that were neatly placed behind me.

Yang was already several feet ahead, though I would have chosen to walk far slower then we was. But, all I could do was follow.

There was this side door. I could tell he was heading for it. So, I slowed my pace down to intermingle a bit more unnoticeable with the early morning airport crowd. But soon, I was outside; linked up with Yang.

Though I attempted to monitor my progress towards the door, I was not sure if *the gang of four* was on my tail.

"We have to leave here, S."
"Why?"
"No time to discuss that, let's go."

We walked down this rather long, semi narrow outdoor pathway. Fenced on one side with metal and wood and concrete. On the other side was the structure.

As we walked, I could not help but think that there was really no way that anybody could know who I was. For I was certain that there was no monitor cameras in that factory that had a bit of an explosion. And, anyone that I would have tapped-up and lived would have been in no condition to give a very accurate description prior to the blast.

I mean, like here I was; now my hair was down—pulled out of its appropriate pony-tailed position, placed as such during the confrontation(s). But still, I looked physically none the worse for the wear. I could have been any tourist.

Then I thought of Yang—maybe they knew him—knew who he was. Maybe it was him that they were after. Then, the box. I thought of the box. Perhaps it was that which they wanted.

Yeah… And, why was I the one who was supposed to take off with it. I mean fuck that! I didn't even know what was inside of it. What a fucked-up thing to lay my direction, you know, *'Like fuck me.'*

We walked on—almost ran. …All of this in mega overdrive. It took place in only a couple of seconds.

Bam! We had turned the corner and ran up against a fence, a locked fence. There was a wooden roof enclosing the gate and surrounding the pathway. Yang turned and looked with eyes full of fear.

It was like a prison cell that he had ran us directly into. There was freedom: the outside, the light. But, there we stood, imprisoned, held back by the inventions of man—like a bird in a cage.

"What do we do now, Yang? Should we go back?"
"No…"

Just as he was saying the word. I heard, in the local tongue.

"Here, give it to me."

It was Ming-zhou, on the outside, not on the inside, not like us.

"Give her the box, S," Yang exclaimed with fear in his voice.
"I understood her," I replied.

He certainly wasn't the warrior that Ming-zhou was. Letting fear overtake you can never be allowed to exist in the mind of the warrior.

"Give it to her!"
"Chill out man."

It's like I almost wanted to say, *"Whoa, cool it dude,"* dialogued in the rap of the seventies. I mean, this dude was mega on—maximum fear overdrive.

I unzipped my leather bag, reached in and slid the box her direction—under the fence. She was gone.

"Let's go back in, man." I said.

Though I could tell that he did not want to, there was little other choice. We proceeded. Just as we turned the corner, there they were a-coming. The white boys and the homeboys. I don't know. I was cool. It was a funny feeling. It's like the thought of anxiety or fear that I had earlier that evening, in the factory, was no longer present. Maybe I was just numb. I don't know. Yang, I could tell; I could feel, was not as adequately prepared.

We were basically out of sight of all the tourist and travelers. Consciously, I checked the scene. They were after us; the four of them. No doubt about that. The cops weren't wearing holsters, (as they do not do in the PRC). But, one was pulling a gun out from behind him. My bag, it now served a purpose. I immediately moved in. I jumped forward; *'SMASH,'* it was in the face of the first white guy. Left leg thrown behind my right, and then one more time, I threw a skipping roundhouse kick right to the face of cop. One down, one out.

The one I passed and introduced to my bag—I did a spinning heel kick to his face. Two down, two out.

The other cop, front kick to the groin, knuckle fist to the solar plexus. Then, a little chiropractic work to his neck.

One final one. A look. A stare. He, like a macho fucking asshole, lunged at me with a punching arm. I side-stepped it, blocked it. Grabbing his hair, pulling his head back, foot to the back of his knee, he was bending down to a more appropriate lower level. With his head yanked back and me towering over him, I looked directly in his eyes—another moment that equaled an eternity. I then delivered a right upward knife hand under his nose. His face was now at my stomach level. I maintained my grasp on his hair. I felt the impact, the blow. I felt the jerk from his body as his soul was instantly set free.

I stood there, holding his hair, lifting his weight. I remained there, holding him, looking at him for a moment. Blood ran from his nose, from his mouth.

Life it is so fragile… Finally, I let him drop.

I turned, looked for Yang. There he was with this small, rather long thin knife. Where that came from, I do not know. He was inserting it into the backside of the necks of those that lay in my wake. I mean like, you know, that slit the throat stuff is all Hollywood. With an assassin, it's in the backside, into the jugular. That way they bleed inside, not like creating an art piece from their blood all over the place.

He was canceling their tickets. I didn't like it. I did not like that chicken shit stuff one bit. That was a *mutha' fucking* bullshit thing to do. Like the sucker punch from behind. I mean, no matter what these dudes point of view may be, a point of view is just that, a set of circumstances, and he was dropping their subscription.

"What the fuck you doing, man?"

He just looked at me as he began to pull his prey over to one side—behind an outcrop of airport junk.

I did not like this shit at all! I mean he didn't back me up, blow-for-blow, in any of it. He was in no way riding shotgun. And, there he was, that little worm, taking these dudes out of the picture. I mean, it wasn't even them or him…

Anyway, I stood there, he pulled them…

"Let's go get on the plane, S."

I begin to walk away, *"Your bag."* He handed it to me.

Back into the line, definitely worse for the wear. We walked on, eventually through the body search and carry on X-ray place. I handed them my bag. It cleared.

I could not help but wonder what it was that had been in that box that Ming-zhou and I had picked up, carried out, at the plant. I mean, what the fuck was this, a set me up to take the fall situation? I mean, I had seen all of those spy movies on T.V., the most expendable one and all. And I didn't really know any of these people—at all. The fucking thoughts raced…

Mostly, I was scared—scared and angry. I mean, I had no place to run. This was not my scene. I had some duped-up passport and some stab in the back confidant. My heart pumped.

The waiting room. I walked in. I had seen it before. I passed through it on a way to some holy destination, a couple of years the previous. A very different time in my life, obviously. Though I didn't realize it until then.

In the waiting room, there was the inside and there was the outside. Some people were here, some were there. I chose to go for the latter; the air, and the fleeting sense of freedom.

*　　*　　*

The sky was gray and full of clouds. People stood around me. People speaking in various dialects. Have you ever realized just how little words really mean? I stood there, breathing deep, trying to figure out just what it was that was happening to me, my life, to the others I had recently come into contact with. What dance of destiny was playing on?

I thought to look for Yang, I didn't trust him at all. I tried to turn but my mind would not let me. It was as if I was bound in the direction of which my eyes found themselves: across the airport, the empty runway(s), the green hills and fields that lay in the distance. I thought to just leave—to go and to run. In actuality, I did not know what to do.

The morning clouds turned to rain. Those around me moved for the inside—the sanctuary of safety. They couldn't see, they didn't understand that it, sanctuary, does not exist. But me, I stood there, content on my view of the distance. My mind in a million places but the here and the now. The rain, I hoped, prayed that it would wash my soul, purge my sins, but I knew it was too late for all that.

My mind went to a time, a lady from distant years past. Once I had asked her, *'Why do you think I choose to pursuit the spiritual in life? Why do I continue to run to the realms where earthly spirituality is at its utmost?'* *'Salvation,'* she said. *'You seek salvation.'*

"Are you alright, S?"

A voice, a touch of my arm. I jumped, ready to pounce. But, it was Yang.

"Yeah, I'm Okay man."
"You had better come inside, you are all wet."
"No, man, just let me be."

I guess he returned to the safety of enclosure.

I watched our plane arrive, late of course. I witnessed the passengers disembark. They ran through the rain, covering themselves with whatever they had: books, purses, and bags. The time, I counted not. I was like on overload. Though I know that I had to realize that I needed to get out-a-there, but that period, it is all so blank.

On the airplane—take off. I sat window seat. I watched the ground fade to the distance. I looked to the structure of the air terminal to see if I could see those whose life we had ended laying there. I watched. I saw nothing. I felt the shaking as we passed through the clouds. I felt freer. I had distance from that place. Freer but yet contained. An airplane inside, it is so small. Outside so large. How do airplanes fly anyway?

*   *   *

I don't know, I guess I had very little sleep of late—I was out.

Dreams: vicious and pounding. I awoke with a gasp for air. I jumped from the realms of sleep to the realms of the living—the awake. The local yokel sitting next to me, my jump, made his jump. He looked at me like I was some sort of *weird-o.* I guess to him I was.

We touched down and though I had full-on paranoia, (I mean did those dead dudes get found), I got off—walked on. This time I was not waiting for Yang. I hit the front door.

Over in the side outer-parking lot, I saw the homeboy of a driver who had met me before. He stood there leaning against his taxi. I walked over to him. He gave me the basic, *"Hellos."* I just opened the door, threw my bag in, and got inside.

Soon, Yang came running up. He looked at me. I gave him that look that could kill. He got in the front seat. Driver entered through the driver side, we drove on.

We pulled up to Bloom's crib, about one or so. He walks out to meet us. He sticks out his hand. I just looked at him, walk by, and hit the inside. He follows me on in. Yang after him. The driver stayed in the car.

"It went well, I hear."
"How can you know that?"

"I have channels, Mr. Storm. Now we have a few days to rest before the secondary part of the assignment."

"We... What the fuck did you do?"

"Yes, I can see you need some rest. I have set up another bed in my room here for you. Why don't you go and take a nap?"

"Why don't I go and take a nap? Why don't you go and fuck yourself! Why the fuck can't you guys spring for a hotel?"

"That is not in the plan, Mr. Storm."

"Well, fuck the plan! I don't go for this roommate bullshit!"

With that, I got up. I walked out to the taxi. I looked back into the house. The crew stood there, they were staring at me through the door.

"Take me to the Hotel X. Don't fucking look at him! Either you take me or I will find another way!"

A nod came from Bloom. I got in the car and the driver took me over to this Five Star, (on the Four Star, in my mind), side of the picture hotel that I cribbed at in this city previously. The driver tried to lay some lingo but I just didn't answer as he stared at me through his rearview mirror. I was just not in the mood.

Up in front of said Hotel X, a doorman catches my door. I walk for the desk, hoping that they had a room for me.

"Hello Dr. Saint James. How have you been? What is it now, a year since we saw you last?"

Fuck, somebody remembered me. I guess I did make quite an impression the last time I stayed here. But that is another story. You can read it in another book.

A million things raced through my mind: what to say, what to do. I didn't have my real passport with me, and come to think of it, *Fuck!*, I didn't have my credit cards either. Man, like you know, I am so used to carrying them, I didn't even think about it. I fumbled for words...

"Do you have a reservation Dr. Saint James?" As she begins to play with the computer.
"Yes. I made it in Hong Kong."
"I do not see that there is anything listed. But, that is no problem Dr. Saint James for we have rooms. How long will you be staying with us?"
"About three days. I will let you know for sure tomorrow."
"Will you be paying for that with your credit card?"
"Uh no. I think I will pay with cash this time."
"That's fine. I see that we have your credit card number on file and since we know you, you will not have to pay in advance."

Man, I lucked out... For even though I did have some local cash that they had set me up with H.K. side. I don't know if it would have even been close to enough to pay for the three days.
'This is a fucking under paid profession,' I thought...

"May I see your passport please?"

I fumbled, I tried to play it off, let her forget, change her mind, but no-go that direction. I finally handed it to her.

"Storm? I thought that your name was Saint James?"
"Well uh, you see, uh, I got married."
"Oh in America, you change the man's name to the lady's name? I never knew that. I thought that it was the other way around."
"Well, it is an old tradition that you can do it either way and her family wanted me to use their name, so I thought that I would be nice and do as they requested."
"Oh, that is so nice. I'm so happy for you that you got married. Congratulation!"

She stared at me for a moment and then giggled. She said, *"I am sure that a few of the young ladies that work here are going to be sorry to hear that. They did have quite a crush on you."* I smiled.

Yeah right, me married... It was an almost unfortunate lie that I had to tell, because I could have sure used some female companionship that evening and I guess that cancelled my chance in that *departmento*. Oh well, hotel staff isn't supposed to link up with the guests anyway. But, I won't tell on the several of them that have with me...

A man came to take my luggage.

"That's it?" He inquired.
"That's it."

He waltzed me up to my room. I slipped him some change for his labor and he left. I put the, *'Do Not Disturb,'* sign on my door.

Solitude. I opened my drapes, stared off into the industry that made up this city. Industry and the side of the hotel which they placed me on. The other side was far more aesthetically pleasing.

I closed the drapes again. I needed silence, both in my ears and visually. Silence in my mind which seemed no longer possible. And I way hoped I hadn't fucked things, namely me, up by checking into this hotel where I was known.

Chapter 15

There came a knock, a knock upon my door. I guess I had been sleeping a long time; a restless long time. And the dreams… Well, I don't want to go into them…

Λ knock again. My thought was to just say, *'Fuck it,'* and not answer at all but the knocking continued. Finally, I pulled myself from between the sheets of passion, grabbed my now dirty and way boring, donated by the company, clothing and pulled them upon my form.

I threw a little peer through the old hotel room door peephole, just to check the *sich;* like was I going to have to duke it out with some local constables or was I going to get blown away, (somewhere safer where the feeling stays), by some other agent operatives on my side of the tracks.

Wow! I looked. I opened the door. It was Ming-zhou.

"Hello S, are you Okay? Mr. Bloom was worried about you."
"When did you come back?"
"Last night. I came back after you and Yang."
"Did you have any problems?"
"No, none."
"What about that box? Did it make it back? And just what was in that box anyway?"
"Can I come in?"
"Oh yeah, sure."

Into the love abode she entered. She stood there tall, in full-on beauty and style. I wished we had met under different circumstances, another time, another way, maybe in some Asian disco. No, that would have been too easy. Maybe an art gallery or maybe in a bookstore. Yes, then it all would have held some cosmic meaning.

She stood. I offered her a place to sit in the dim light of the day that barely found its way through the drawn light brown drapes.

Conversation was strained. I didn't know what to say to her. It had all been too intense. And I was still way too cranked from it all. But there she sat, *my comrade in arms.* She had fought next to me, with style and passion. I next to her. And all for what? Some stupid political realm of political bullshit that certainly I didn't even come close to understanding or caring about. People had died...

"Let's go out S. There is this place that I would like to take you."
"Where?"

All the thoughts of paranoia flashed in my mind. Had I worn out my usefulness? Was it that I had bailed Bloom's house and went off to stay on my own? Were they going to take me out of the picture in some dark and removed lo-cal?

The thought of lust, the dude in me came out, as well. There she was, this babe of babes, sitting in my love crib central. Could I have her? Maybe...

Well, what could I say, what could I do? If my number was up, and with an organization such as this, I doubted that there was much that I could do to escape. So, I went along for the ride...

*   *   *

As she waited, as she watched, I changed into my third and last set of company issued clothing: brown cotton pants, a green shirt, and a khaki colored sport jacket. The rest of the stuff, I put out in front of the door and gave the old laundry service a ring on the tele. We, she and I, left.

On the way down, past the coffee shop, I suggested a little on the breakfast side of the picture. She agreed. And though, I think it made me more sick to my stomach than anything else, I guess the session was enjoyable enough, surrounded by the lame tourists, the high-end locales, and mostly a whole lot of people staring and wanted to figure out just what this babe and I were a-doing—doing breakfast to-get-her. Fuck 'em.

Out to the outside, met by the local employed by the company driver. Funny, I didn't really feel like looking at him. I suggested that we just take a local taxi wherever it was that we were going but Ming-zhou insisted against that. Which naturally sent my movements of paranoia into action again. Was that breakfast to be my last supper?

In to the car. The eyes of the masses were upon her and upon me. Same old story of the babes and me in Asia. They, the locals, the tourists, and the peeps in general, they are all just jealous.

Well, we both got into the back and the guy drove off. He tried to lay a little rap my direction but I was in no mood.

"Where are we going?"
"Mr. Bloom says that you are from California. I know that California has a beach and I know that

101

you must be homesick. So, I want to show you our beach."

"Homesick, no. I never get homesick. But hey, seeing a beach sounds good to me. I love the ocean. I think few people love it more than I..."

The drive took us out of the town and on to the highways; such as they are in this non-descript region of discussion.

We drove past the city into the country, where the people lay their rice on the road to be run over by the passing cars in order to break off the husks. Looks pretty unsanitary to me, but...

The people were simple though, you know. You could see that their existence was just a day-to-day ritual of survival. Of eating, sleeping, working, and the etc. It is no wonder that individual mysticism had shut down in that country. I mean, like there was no time for internal reflection.

'The sad story of the world' I thought. *'No time to think, to live, to experience. Only time to work and deal with the mundane.'*

These people we drove past obviously had no idea of what was going on—of what had gone on in my life in the last couple of days. Of what had gone on with/and of the respective governments involved. Of which mine, the good old U.S.A. was deeply involved to whatever covert degree.

The people, they just grew their food, worked their fields of rice, had no idea of the folly of the world: fashion-passion, style, money, fame, and governmental power.

I always thought that life was backwards. I mean like, everyone goes to school, gets a job, works until they are sixty-five, retires, and dies. I mean, by the time they retire they are too old to do

102

anything anyway. I think it should be the other way around: live, party until you are sixty-five and then go and get a job. Live while you can really enjoy it!

Sorry to deviate. Back to the story…

We drove. I witnessed. As we moved through the country, Ming-zhou sat closer to me, leg-to-leg, she leaned against me. She took my hand. I held hers. And, for a moment, it was the pure embrace of total ecstasy. Eventually, she lay her head on my shoulder and fell asleep.

I felt so close to her. Like she knew and understood my soul. Though so few words had even ever been spoken between us, it was not important. Of all that had gone down, all that had transpired, she was the only person I had an ounce of respect for. And then she was asleep on my shoulder.

The embrace of unknown personality, of known self was almost too much to handle. It was like all my fear, my anger, my anxiety from the days before was being lifted from inside of me and being placed in the fire of the Hindu god, *Angi*— burned to a crisp where it just no longer mattered anymore.

*   *   *

As we pulled up to this place, it did not look much like the beach to me. There were a few cars around and what looked to be some sort of raised roof, hidden behind a gate. I kinda gave Ming-zhou a bit of a nudge and she jumped to full-on awake.

"Oh, we are here," she exclaimed.

So, out of the car we get and on she leads us forward. The driver told her in their native dialect that he would pull around the south side and chill back.

We walked through this gate. She laid down the fee that had to be paid in the direction of the keeper of said gate.

"What is this place?"
"It's a very old temple."
"Looks pretty new to me."
"They have refurbished it."

Inside, I laughed at her choice of words, *'Refurbished...'*

We walked around a bit. Pulled in on a local movie crew that was filming a movie. The cast the crew, they all threw a look my direction. *'Oh maybe I will be discovered and I can be a star.'* They just went back to work. Oh well...

Chapter 16

The embrace, the touch, the hold, I could not let my mind drift any further. If this was the death that I had worried about, then let me die here, in the arms, in the body of love.

The sky pounded in its perfection. The sun touched me. They sky, the sun, they brought to us just the perfect amount of fragrant intensity. God, the feelings of love. The pounding, the pulsing of the heart. We were way-way too on. I made love to her as if my life depended on it. In fact, it did, for I was no longer sure what the next moment may bring.

As we lay there in the sand, the green almost pink, almost circular vegetation painted soft colors, as my eyes would momentarily open to study her enjoyment, understand her experience.

"I love you S."
"I love you too, Ming-zhou."

*   *   *

the wind it can dance on our souls
as it gently blows through our hair
and the sun may burn home its passion
bleeding its warmth down deep into our hearts
> *life, it will love*
> *life, it will die*
and illusion it may take hold of us
as desires may imprison our minds
but when all of it comes together
if only for a second
for only a moment can it last
then life all falls into its own perfection

and all that is being had
is all that was ever wanted
and the dripping of time
that is measured
by the incoming waves of the sea
it passes through the hands of God
like the grains of sand upon which we lie
and it all will equal nothing
not anything at all

as the sun shines
as the waves move
as two bodies embrace one another in perfection

as the wind gently blows
to its own unknown destiny
held back by nothing
moving to its own reason

for there is no wind through the trees
on a treeless beach

*   *   *

I would never have chosen to leave that zone of pleasure with her. I would never have chosen to leave that spot. For in her arms, in her body, I came to know everything. Everything—perfection within itself.

The world though, like the working rice farmers, like the businessmen, like the spies, were are all bound by something; no matter how much we attempt to escape that fact. But, me, too—me too... I was bound.

"Mr. Storm, Mr. Storm. Ming-zhou, Ming-zhou,"

We hear a voice calling out to us. Our driver, no doubt.

A last note on the subject, God was that session of love intense. Man, was it love.

So, a long story made too long or too short, I do not know—I don't have that answer. We got our clothing together. I helped her brush off. Didn't want the dude to get any of the wrong ideas. We made our way up the little hill. He wanted to bail, was worried that we would get back too late. As seems to forever be the case, the death of perfection is brought about my the hands, by the mind of another...

As we drove back, the looks, the glances that Ming-zhou continued to pour upon me were like way far too lovingly intense. Like every time I would look her way, there they were, being pasted over me like peanut butter. And even through my peripheral vision, I could see her with this little smile of love upon her lips, glistening in my direction. Man, I felt it too.

*   *   *

Well anyway, enough of all this sensitivity bullshit. You will think that I am some kind of a wimp.

She eventually fell asleep on my shoulder as hand-in-hand we drove back to the city. She had to have been way burned out from all that had been going down. No doubt she was obviously way more versed in the subject than I. But, none-the-less...

Back at love crib central, I invite her to dinner. Though the *dweeb* driver gave some responses to the *nagatory* over the suggestion. I

107

told him straight out that it was none of his fucking business and to go take a hike. I could tell Ming-zhou dug all my *macho* bullshit. But, anyway…

So, we did the basic dinner in the expensive dining room, up topside on the love shack. Signed my name, like you know, *'Put it on the tab.'* The tab that I had not figured out how I was going to pay.

We did the basic stare into each other's eyes; hold hands under the table, and all that. Oh yeah, I wasn't going to rap about the LOVE stuff anymore. *Sorry*…

Back to the room. There was no longer even a question if she would accompany me or not. We lay around and held each other and kissed for a time. Ming-zhou suggested the taking of a shower. Which I mean, *'Hey,'* that's like right up my alley. The old take a shower, soap up each other's bodies, and rub against one another, while the sexual healing be-a *tak'n* place.

We did a bit of *mak'n* love in the shower. Quite a bit more in between the sheets.

I am trying to go for the PG audience here and am not going to be too explicit as my books based on my life tend to be. So, just tune in your imagination, or pick up another one of my more descriptive texts to understand what my LOVE technique(s) would have been.

Eventually, we fell off to sleep in one another's arms.

Chapter 17

It must have been morning. It woke me from my sleep. The telephone, that is, it rang.

"Is Ming-zhou there?"
"Yes."
"Can I speak with her?"

I knew it was Yang, that little weasel of a counter espionage agent.

"Why? Talk to me."

He reluctantly went into the rap that the car would be waiting and we must go to Bloom's immediately. I told him to fuck off and hung up. I mean with love in my arms, I was in no mood for anything but the said.

Ming-zhou, however, far more dedicated or maybe just more scared of the possible *what-could-happen* if she didn't immediately respond than I. She, she jumped up and prepared to go—once she was told of the conversation.

"Why, let's just hang out here."
"We must go S. We must!"

As she prepared her body for the day's activities to come, she looked at me,

"S, I cannot take this anymore. When this assignment is over, will you take me away with you?"

I didn't even have to answer. We both knew the answer was, *"Yes."*

We bailed. Yeah, the car, the driver he was waiting, complete with the negative vibes and his obvious dislike of our love connection. Well, fuck him.

We got to Bloom's. Blooms met us outside.

He wanted us in *pronto. 'This was the time,'* so he said. We had to move in on our secondary target NOW. They were apparently anticipating another attack and were fortifying their defenses. If we didn't go now, right now, there would be no way to penetrate them.

"But this is fucking daylight, Bloom!"
"That's good, they will not expect an attack."

He laid down the basic plan of attack. Showed us the map, the explosive components and all.

We were all going in. All of us. None left on the outside to pick up the pieces, should they begin to fall. No back up. *No nada.* He wanted me to go in with Yang.

"No fucking way, man! I do not like his style!"

It was resolved; I would head in with him, Bloom—the main and local head *honcho.*

I didn't like that much better. But, it/the situation was like being in bed with dick hard, dick in, and ready to blow the cookies in a woman that you know you shouldn't *cum* in for she may get knocked-up. But, like there just is just no fucking way in the world that you can pull out. So, you do

110

it. Blow the cookies and let the cards of destiny fall where they may.

Ming-zhou, she would go in with Yang. I didn't like that much either but the move, it was in motion.

Chapter 18

The car drove on. Bloom and I, we were riding back side in one car, Yang and Ming-zhou in another. The city, modern, yet an air of the primitive radiated from within its bounds: the stone house, the factories, the graying sky—like some gothic painting or some gothic music, like something, I know not what.

"Why are you so against Yang?"
"Because he's a mutha' fucking snake. He killed people when there was no reason to do it. And when it was down to the fight, he was not riding shotgun at all. It was me and no one else."
"You have to try to understand Yang. There is a lot of things that he went through that you just do not know about or understand."
"Well, that is his fucking business, just keep him the fuck away from me. I do not trust the mutha' fucker."

I was in a bad mood, a bad space. I was being walked straight up to the door of death again and I seriously had no desire to be there. I wanted to just tell everyone to, *'Fuck off'* and like bail the whole fucking scene with Ming-zhou and live happily ever after somewhere, with some white picket fence. But like any man with no tears—I walked on into the abyss. And, fuck me if I would bail like a pussy or go down without a fight.

"So, I hear you caught a little trim off of Ming-zhou. How'd you pull that one off? Promise her something? I've been after that for quite awhile."
"Fuck you, man."

112

I was about to go up-side his bitch head. I just did not need to hear that kind of shit at all. But, I understood the gravity of our situation, so I chilled. I looked out of the window. I tried to breathe deep. Personally, I just wanted to kill that fat asshole.

He didn't say another word but me. I was like a fucking boiling kettle ready to explode.

The drive of an hour or so went slow. I could not still my thought patterns.

*   *   *

We approached. I had in my possession three of the explosive devices, previously described, as used by Ming-zhou. I was to go in from one position. From my recollection and positioning on the map, it appeared to be from the North.

The target, another chemical weapons factory, it stood alone and isolated, out in the distance. It was large. Grass fields surrounded it. The gray sky pasted it rock hard against the horizon. Me, I though of Ming-zhou. I thought of the love we made. I thought of the beach that we lay in each other's arms upon. I questioned, *'Would I ever know her love again?'*

I was to be let off. We pulled in, too close I thought; a dirt road. They stopped near a tree. Gray, all I saw was gray: the factory, the sky, and the stacks that poured clouds into the air.

"Ming-zhou and Yang have probably already penetrated the perimeter. We will be entering soon. Check your watch; be out of there by 3:30, for that is when the detonators will go off. Remember meet

us on the far side from here, at the transportation depot."
"Fuck you," I said, as I got out of the car.

They drove off. I stood by the tree for a few moments; several I guess. I looked; there was no noticeable human movement. Only the billowing of clouds of chemical smog finding its way into the pure China sky.

* * *

Yeah right, this was for the safety of the world. The bullshit world, the political powers who love to jack off and think that they are doing something for one purpose or another, only to be undermined by another political strength. Like you know, no matter how big and bad you be, there is always someone bigger and bad-er.

* * *

I stood up straight—up off the tree I had been leaning upon. It made me think of my younger days, of monkhood, nature, India, and the dream. Yeah, the dreams they were so simple back then; simple things for a non-materialistic person. Damn, life has gotten confusing.

I walked towards the fence. I was maybe fifty yards away. Closer, I began to notice something—something not right. Upon it, the fence, I checked to be sure. Yeah, the fucking thing was electric. How the fuck was I supposed to get over this?

I WAS FUCKING BOILING! I knew Bloom had set it up this way, so I would either be

114

killed or look like I had not done my assignment. Man, I was fucking mad. It made me want to do this thing more, so I could just get to Bloom and blaze that bitch up.

I looked around for a method in. Holes, no way. Pole vault, that's a joke. I remember this spy movie, back from when I was a kid, about how this one dude had flipped a ladder up the side of an electric fence and kinda see-sawed it over. But, I was a little bit low in the teeter-tauter department.

Finally, down the fence a bit, a few hundred yards, I saw a tree. This one branch looked to be going over, just enough. I would have to take a closer look.

I walked the fence, kinda ran. I saw the road and the occasional passing vehicle, several hundred yards to my right. The factory grounds, empty. I mean like, where were all the people that should be patrolling this bad boy? Maybe they were just waiting for me to hop over and then nail me with the big guns. I mean, it was fuck me in every direction.

I got up to the tree. Yeah, if I did it right, I could climb up, hop over, and be in. But once in, there was no way out. At least not the way I came in.

It was like I was staring down the throat of death. I just wanted to walk away...

I got to thinking about things, you know: Bloom, Yang, the assignment, and all. That *mutha' fucker* Bloom had given me the worst way in. The most exposed. Obviously, the most deadly. He would get rid of me and get the assignment done. He would come out the winner. Me, I was expendable, I would be dead.

Man, I just wanted to get this done, so I could put down that asshole Bloom. Put him down, get Ming-zhou, and never, never, never again let myself be bought like a cheap high-heeled whore on a Saturday night.

I climbed up the tree. I shimmied out to the branch. My small bag with the explosives was in the way, but I had no choice than to bring them along. Out on the edge, I realized that to clear that fence I was going to have to make a serious jump. Which meant that I was going to have to, more-or-less, stand up on this non-too thick branch to make said jump. I was not happy.

More than anything else, the thought of Ming-zhou rang in my brain. Yeah, I know, I am a fool; falling in love and all of that, but I had to do this or look like a coward, feel like a coward, forever. And, that was just not me.

I got out as far as I could, to still have enough branch to be able to repel off of. I kinda got to my feet, holding on to one of the other branches. I tossed the bag. Well, it made it…

For me, it was like being on a high dive board and you are not quite sure that you want to dive and go into the water—I mean it is so fucking high and all. Maybe it would be better to just climb down the diving board ladder and go home. But, then you look like a puss. I could not do that.

I had to stop myself from thinking. I kept telling myself that… But, I kept thinking.

Finally, I just threw myself and jumped. It was close, way close. It's like I could feel the electricity from the fence breathe on me. But, I was on the ground and still not fried.

I grabbed the bag, expecting to be shot at any second. I ran, as low to the ground as possible, in true GI style—the way I had seen in all of the movies. I wondered if there were landmines or something planted and soon I would be toast, upon placing my next step. Was that why there weren't any noticeable guards? But, all I could do was to keep running.

As I approached the building, I startled a bird that had landed and was *chill'n* on the ground. He flew off.

I had not noticed the bird. My heart jumped with him.

But again, with his flight, I was reminded of the freedom, the dream…

But, there is just no place to dream, when your life is up against the wall, and any move could be your last.

I made it to the building. There were no windows, no doors on my side. I had to figure out a way to get in.

I ran the wall, looking, cussing, becoming more-and-more pissed at Bloom, with every step.

I hit a right angle. I came up to a corner. I carefully looked around said corner. I surmised that this was the side of the building that the main entrance gate was on—for I could see it in the distance. I also saw a door, a small door, a bit up ahead. It looked to be some sort of service entrance or a place for the workers to catch a breather.

My thoughts of going back the other way and seeing what may be to the other side, the far side of the building, the side without the main entrance gate, the side where there were not at least a dozen armed men guarding said gate came to a halt as I looked at my watch, 2:44. No time to fuck around.

I looked; no one was looking my way. I strolled, cool and slow, approached the door. I walked up the three or four steps of the small metal porch that protruded from its entrance. I turned around, scoped the *sich,* looking as *au-casual* as possible. Still no one picking up on my vibes.

I tried the door. First turn of the metal handle it did not move. Like a million lifetimes in one second, I knew that it was locked. I tried again, with a bit more animal force. It turned and it opened. I, in all my style entered, like in the best of the Bruce Lee movies, with my fist clinched and ready.

There was no one there for it to be introduced to it, however. I was in.

The gray sky no longer reminded me of the old black and white horror movies. Inside, I had walked into a hall, gray and white, metal and stone, not so different from the previous plant, which I had visited. I saw no movement. I walked forward.

My mission was to locate these three mechanical contraptions: two chemical vats and one power converter. They had been described to me well enough at our little *powwow* over the map in Bloom's crib, as well as their approximate *lo-cal.* I was a bit turned around having entered from a different angle than had been described by Bloom.

Bloom; thinking about him, I was pissed off again. Thinking about him lead me to thinking about Yang. You know how thoughts are… Yeah, I should have taken that asshole Yang with me and then I would not be riding this boat solo. But, all that I had was me. Me, I trusted myself. I did not trust him.

And though the nervousness pumped in me—you know, like that all alone kind of nervousness. I was on, and I had to get this done, if for no other reason then to tap up that *mutha' fucker* Bloom.

I knew that I needed to walk into a more central area to find the centrally located vats of disaster. So, I moved on.

I walked the hall, well halls. Opened a wood door here, a metal door there. I tried to enter into the central factory.

I had not passed anyone, which made me *mucho* nervous. That was until I powered on through this one door and was clear and full-on in chemical warfare factory central.

There was movement, a lot of movement. I guess this was why there was no one on the outside; they were all wrapped up tight on the inside. I didn't really know what the people were doing. It looked like they were taking things down or apart or something. In truth, I knew so little about this whole operation, but something was going on. Like maybe, they were pulling all of the chemicals out or changing something, or like I don't know?

The people, again they were mostly all white homeboys, so I blended in. I did not stop to look or to take much notice. I moved on/moved through.

I had entered into/onto this metal scaffolding that rose above the base of the plant. The plant, which surged down below me. I could look to a distance; see a structure that seemed to go on forever. This was one way-big place. I could not even see where it ended.

There were all kinds of metal vats, piping going fucking everywhere, planks, panels, and people, moving mega fast.

As I walked, I calculated the vat I was to have to come in on. I checked, I viewed, and to the best of my abilities, I scooped what looked to be the three bad pups I was to take down. I, how shall I say, moved in their direction.

I walked passed a few people, to no notice, as I went down the metal stairs. Onto the floor, still no notice. There was a lot of action, people strutting by me in every direction, a few forklifts, with some kegs of, *I could only guess what,* and talk, a lot of talk.

I strolled up to target one. It towered above me in all of its metal circular shape-ness. The bomb, it was planted.

I walked on over to two, slid it in on the side, so no notice could be taken of it. Three, a bit farther up, tall and cylindrical. It was done. I was in the mode of bail. *'This was all way too easy,'* I thought. Easy, it made me nervous.

I calculated the direction of the motor pool where we were all to meet. I headed that way. Up some metal stairs, to the side, this way and that.

*   *   *

The dream, it was going to be a reality; the dream of the love I had come to know just a few short moments ago. The dream, the love, the way into to the way out, all consummated on this beach, now far in the distance.

Me, I will have served my country. I will have helped the Free World. I will have paid back some of my debt. I was soon to be out—soon to be free. I picked up my pace, the dream it was in sight.

RING! Bip, bap, and boo. I mean like how do you describe in words the sound of a massively loud alarm going off. It hit me hard. Like a sucker punch from the rear. Like a knife in the fucking heart.

I looked around; there was definite panic in the air. I was not sure what, but something had gone wrong in the plant. Was it me? Or, had one of my *compatriots* been discovered?

I could not panic. I had to hold it tight, keep it together, and just make my move for my described exit.

I was cruising down a hall. It was a small hallway that fed from the main hall to the central area of chemical battle. Out of the corner of my eye, peripheral vision, there he was latched up in combat. Him and one, two, three, maybe four. Yang was into it.

My first though was to just say, *'Fuck 'em'* and move on. For I fit in, bended well with my *Anglo* surroundings.

I thought of how that *puto* had sucker *stived* those people in the neck. That was no way to fight a war. No way for a solider to behave. I thought to leave, but I could not bring myself to do it.

In a glance, Yang eyes met mine. I ran down the hall, towards him. I blew through the several guys around him, fist first. I caught the guy that was hammering on Yang; my fist right in his temples. He went down. My elbow came back and whammed on the face of the next nearest target. Yang jumped up and began to throw some lame *Southern Kung Fu* moves, that did nothing but get him punched up some more. I threw a foot here, a hand there, I was holding my own, but there was more homeboys a-coming.

It is a hard thing to explain in the middle of a fight, the view, and the scene. I mean like, because you see your immediate opponent, and the next one, and the next one to come. It is kind of like a chess game, a game where only one can come out the winner. In this view, in this spectrum, I saw it happening. I do not remember where this opponent was placed in my list of oncoming attacks, but he was in there. In there and on Yang. As I spun to back kick one of the punks, I watched as the knife, a large one, military black Kbar type, enter straight into the stomach of Yang. I saw his Asian eyes close with a scream of endings. It was over. His ticket was cancelled.

I banged it out a bit more, but with him *out-a-there* and the onslaught of adversaries coming, it was my time to exit stage left. I front kicked this one guy under the jaw and jumped back. I ran through a nearby door. The swinging double door, well one of them anyway, served a temporary purpose as my hand found its way around it and directed it into the oncoming face of some homeboy. It pushed him back just enough to give me a moment to run. And, run I did.

I was chased, naturally. But, I don't know; aside from a few *'quick stop,'* turn and wait for a follower or two to turn the corner and run face-first into one of my punches or kicks, I seemed to be getting away from my chasers pretty rapidly. I guess I had a bit more adrenalin going in my favor.

I was running, trying to get out. I mean this place was going to blow.

Through another one of those double doors, I came face-to-face with this big *hombre* of a *mutha' fucker.* My fate was sealed. No way in, no way out. But damn, this felt so fucking good. It was like pure energy, dynamic power. I wanted him. That *mutha' fucker* was mine.

122

I came right at him; roundhouse punched him right across the nose. Staggered that big *mutha' fucker.* Then a pure uppercut under his jaw. Man, my fists felt good. Then I kicked him, right, square, in the balls, grabbed his head, and shoved it into my knee. I threw that bitch's ass onto the floor.

"Remember who your fucked with, mutha' fucker," I said that to him as I bailed on.

Out of the hall, I kept moving. I was not really sure to where.

As the alarm, alarmed on, I slowed down, walked on, trying to lay low, blend in. Occasional people passed me unnoticed in the hall. I came to this one large room—large but emptier, not the factory central.

There it was. I saw it, the exit. I made my way for it—passed a local or three, hit the handle, and I was out.

I looked around. I was high—high up above the ground. It was a platform in all of its metal-ness.

As I studied the view, there was a jerk, a vibration. I turned, ready to fight. But, it was just my head, no one was after me. I looked at the scene: gothic, very-very metal and gothic, painted against the gray sky.

No time to admire the aesthetics, however, I had to bail. I looked; yes, there was the motor pool. Down the metal stairs I went. I hit the ground running

It was a few hundred yards away from the main structure. Closer to it was this rather rusty silver metal hanger looking building. I bobbed and weaved my way in its direction. I looked at my watch, 3:23.

123

I got to the gate. There were no apparent workers on the premises. I walked in.

Like a junkyard, like a grease pit, it smelled of *auto-mobil* decay. There were trucks, cars, even a cycle or three. Some old, some new, some rusty. It was all like death warmed over.

"Mr. Storm, come here!"

There was Bloom by a car. A red and running car. I made my way his direction.

"Yang's dead, man. They knifed him up on the inside. I don't know if he got his stuff done."
"That doesn't matter now, we have to go!"
"What about Ming-zhou? Where is she?"
"We have to go Mr. Storm."
"Where the fuck is Ming-zhou!"

I grabbed the fat fuck by the arm.

"They have her too, Mr. Storm. There was nothing that I could do. I don't think that she is dead, but we have to go now."

He grabs me by the arm and tries to pull me.

"Fuck you, man!"

I push him away. I don't really know where I was planning to go or what I was planning to do. It was just pure emotion that sent me into a rage. He tried to grab me again, I shoved him away again and for a moment I thought to hit him, punch him, knock the *mutha' fucker* out. I thought all that in the space of a second, when, all-of-a-sudden, *'Wham,'* he sweep kicked me and as I was going down. I felt the embrace of his fist into my jaw. He was a lot faster than a fat man should be.

On the ground I tried to take him down with my legs, tried to lock his knees. He jumped back too fast. I rolled back on the fucking greasy ground, giving me just enough time to get up. As I was doing so, I sensed a foot coming my direction, right at face level. I blocked it as best as I could but the impact sent my arm into my face. I was back down on my butt.

Now I was really pissed. I jumped up; first forward and caught him in the jaw. *'BAM'* then came my left. You know like, *'I got one fist of iron, the other of steel, if my left one don't get you, then my right one will.'*

He was backed up a bit. I swung a roundhouse kick to his face. He blocked it some, but like the kick that hit me, it sent him flying back onto the ground.

I was about to go at him hard but the explosion hit. It was like a nuclear attack. *'BAM!'* I mean like, the sky was colored with red and yellow paint. It sent me to the ground.

Bloom was getting up. I was getting up. I was up first. I tossed a spinning heel kick to his head, I placed it on the right side of his face, just so he would know where I was a-coming from. He went down again. Just then, the driver came from behind me, I saw him coming as I spun and he tried to grab me in a full nelson.

"Don't grab me, mutha' fucker! Just do not try to fuck with me!"

I pulled loose. He went to get Bloom. He carried him into the car. He looked at me. Was I getting in? Fuck! What else could I do? The factory was toast.

We got into the car. We drove out the strategically placed rusting gate to the main highway.

I sat there, as we drove, witnessing this entire blaze of glory into the reigning sky. I could not stop thinking of Ming-zhou, was she in there, had she left this planet, gone from the reach of my grasp forever? I even tossed a selfish though my direction, *'Damn, I hope all of the chemical shit doesn't leak out and chill all over my bones.'*

*   *   *

Bloom didn't say anything the whole ride. He rode shotgun in the front seat. I rode in the back. We finally got back to his crib. The car stopped. We got out. I began to walk away.

"It would be much better if you stayed here S."
"Just find out about Ming-zhou. Call me. I'll go in and get her out whereever she is!"

I walked on, caught a taxi to my hotel. And though I was a bit ashamed of the condition of my khaki colored clothing, I walked through the lobby, gave a glance of hello or three, and moved on up the elevator and into my room.

I lay there that night, waiting, wanting, every thought, every vision going to Ming-zhou. Where was she, had she, could she have made it out? There was no room for sleep. There could only be visions of all the horror that had happened the last few days and of all the love that transpired on the beach within her arms in only a few brief moments.

I lay there, heaven and hell, love and war. The bed we made love in. The room that was our first home and the fucking stupid political battle which raged on just outside my door.

*   *   *

I laid out in the room for the night. I saw the morning sun come through the drapes. There had been no knocks on the door. There had been no telephone calls.

Showered and dressed, I headed for Blooms. Inside he exclaims,

"How could you have brought an average taxi here S. Don't you realize that could expose the whole operation?"

I ignored him and his nonsensical statement. Firmly, I inquired, *"What about Ming-zhou?"*

He looked into the vague distance of the house walls. I could see he did not want to answer. I knew I did not want to hear what he had to say.

"They took her from the factory before it exploded..." He stated. I waited. *"She is probably dead by now S. The last word from my sources is that they started with her fingers; they cut them off one at a time to get her to reveal what she knows. Then they moved onto to her feet, her legs. She told them nothing..."*

127

I don't know, maybe I cried. I do know I threw over his table, smashed his chairs. Maybe I screamed, I don't quite remember. Looking back, I know I lost something in that moment, something that I could never regain.

For all the political movements, all the demi-gods who hold power for a second and think they are something—they are all truly nothing.

Belief is nothing. Power is nothing. Religion is nothing. All those things do is kill people—people like Ming-zhou. Kill them all for nothing. Because all the powers, all the religions, all the politics, they all go away. Sooner-or-later they are all gone.

And, anybody dying for them is never worth the price. What they have to offer was never worth her life. And nothing that they could say and nothing that I could do would ever, ever change that.

I don't know, I kinda walked out of there, bailed on for the airport. I had enough bucks to get me a ride back H.K. direction. And, you know like, on the flight all I could see was her. All I could feel was nothing. But, all I could think, *'Was this the karmic payment I received for all the lives I had taken on this journey, all the husbands, lovers, sons, that would never return home.'*

No, nothing is ever worth death.

*   *   *

Back in H.K. I motored on to the flat. They were not surprised to see me. I guess Bloom must have sent word that I was *en route*.

I entered the flat. Everything was in order. All of my clothing had been dry-cleaned. My shirts, my pants, my suits hung in the closet. Everything else was neatly folded in the drawers. My passport and wallet were placed upon the bedroom dresser. I lay back for that night, got my shit together and the next morning I walked on.

The phone rang as I left. I did not answer it. Downstairs the doorman caught me and told me that Mr. Dozer had tried to contact me. He said that we needed to speak.

"Anything that he wants from me he can just send a request to my P.O. Box back in L.A."

The driver, the friendly bad lad, was positioned out in front of the place. All smiles, he met me and was opening the door for me. I got in.

"How are you Dr. Saint James?"
"Take me to the airport."
"I can't do that. I have to take you to the office, sir."

I didn't say a word. I got out, walked down the street, and grabbed a taxi. With my credit cards in hand, I booked the afternoon flight to Bangkok. The place where illusion reigns supreme and the elixir promised a moment of forgetfulness.

S.
The Oriental Hotel
Bangkok, Thailand
89.18.9